The Launch

A Novel

By Mark Victor Young

Featuring Comic Strips Written by Mark Victor Young
And Drawn by Tim Levins

Copyright

The Launch by Mark Victor Young

Featuring original comic strips written by Mark Victor Young and drawn by Tim Levins.

Published by **Hanton House Creative Media** in London, Ontario, Canada.

First print edition November 2015

ISBN: 978-0-9938558-7-0

Enquiries: info@hantonhouse.com

Cover Artwork by Tim Levins at http://timlevins.deviantart.com/

For all the wives
who have to put up with this shit.

one

My name is Watson Sinclair and I am a pathetically heterosexual man. Not the kind who decides in elementary school that he likes girls but is too shy to do anything about it all the way through high school, learning what he can from teen romance books, pornography and playground rumors, although that, too. Compulsive ogling is the true symptom of my condition. Unsubtle rubbernecking is its unfortunate result. I have always lived in fear that I would see some particularly attractive woman while driving and be so distracted that I'd just drive my car up onto the sidewalk, probably uncorking a fire hydrant or something. This has never happened to me until now.

The particularly attractive woman who has so completely bamboozled my powers of concentration is radically under-dressed for the weather and is probably running across the street from her office or something. Tight black skirt, black tights and long spiky heels in the snow, but no coat. She has long dark hair, creamy skin flushed from the cold and a low-cut shirt with excellent cleavage. As I'm realizing that I have run up into a sidewalk fruit stand, she's turning a corner and now there's a Korean guy yelling at me and waving a broom.

Forgetting that you're driving a car to stare at a woman who hasn't given you the slightest provocation is pretty sick. What is even sicker is that seeing all this fruit on the ground, I can't help thinking that her boobs are at least as big as these large navel oranges, maybe even the grapefruits. And speaking of headlights, I've got no time to sit around picking citrus out of my grill. I was only supposed to drive around the block a few times and come back and now this damn calamity.

I peel off a couple of twenties and drop them on top of the pile of fruit in the snow. I jump back in the front seat, slamming and then locking the door just as the broom hits home on the window. Thank God the front of the car was nose deep in wooden stalls or he'd have come at me straight instead of having to circle around the back. I give him a polite wave and smile even though his spittle is flecking my window as he shouts incoherently. And all this because I am a goggle-eyed tongue loller who can't look away from T&A. Normally I rely on my best friend and artistic partner, JC Dubois, to say "Eyes on the road, Watson," but he is currently a few blocks away, kidnapping the Editorial Director of the Royal Features Syndicate.

I honk my horn and pull back into traffic. Yes, I'm Canadian and a crazy driver: deal with it. It has to be the stress of driving in this metropolitan mayhem that short-circuited my brain into looking for some comforting eye candy.

Focus, Watson. I'm in Midtown near the park and I have to get back to the Royal Features building. I drove past the MOMA two blocks ago and I got stuck in traffic for a while, then I saw Carnegie Hall at one point. If I can make it there, I know I can get back to where I started. Damn these Manhattan one way streets. I can't stop to ask for directions, because I just know when I ask how to get to Carnegie Hall, some hilarious New Yorker will say "Practice."

Speaking of Big Apple clichés straight out of a Woody Allen film, there are yellow taxis just everywhere. I think they see the Ontario plates and jump all over me like a lion on a gazelle. I hate to think what their insurance rates must look like, because I have stomped on the binders more times in the last five minutes than I have since my renewal. If JC texts me right now, I'm in trouble.

Finally, there's an oldster asleep at the switch. Muscle the nose of the car into this small gap, cue honking, now flip him the bird while inching into the space I've created. There. I'm moving again and the old guy is back there miming the "storm on the heath" scene from King Lear. Man, he is *coming apart*. I guess you get used to this eventually.

Through a patch of daylight between buildings I can see the Rockefeller Center. Fifth Avenue is coming up. I'm on East 55th Street heading west, which sounds strange, but I know this will get me back to Seventh Avenue, which will get me down to Carnegie Hall. We went over these maps fifty times, and thank God we did. Traffic is actually moving along a bit, so I'm in good position. What is taking JC so long?

The last time either of us planned and executed a crime was when we were twelve. We ran a complicated distraction technique. JC asked the shopkeeper how much were the dusty boxes of 35mm film up on a high shelf and I swiftly pocketed two chocolate bars and exited the store. We felt guilty about it in the parking lot afterward because the guy who ran the store was really nice and that was the end of our career as criminals. Until now.

As I'm changing lanes to turn right onto Seventh Avenue, I hear a bicycle bell chiming at me urgently. This is it. I pick up my cell phone just to confirm he's ready for pickup.

The eagle has landed.

That JC. Always quick with a book reference. I didn't think my adrenal system could work any harder. My out-of-province health insurance would cover a heart attack, but it would really slow us down right now. I make the turn onto Seventh and hurry up and wait for the light. Come on green, I know you can do it. I can see the damn building. JC and his "patient" Ray are probably waiting for the elevator right now, which is all good. But if they make it to the ground floor and are standing around with no "ambulance" in sight, it will look pretty suspicious. The traffic begins to surge forward hesitantly with the changing of the light, inertia giving way to the perpetual motion of the city. I'm just focusing on the bumper in front of me. I am not my urgency. It is outside of me like a weather system. I am only energy and drift, and this traffic is a pattern of slowly developing possibilities that ebb and flow with my breathing.

Thank God for my yoga training! My heartbeat is under control and I'm back in front of the building where I dropped JC off. I park the car and put on the 4-ways. Pop the locks again just to make sure. The wheelchair door springs open and out roll the feet of my nemesis, pushed along by JC in a wheelchair marked "Patient Transfer."

Ray's head is slumped to the side and he's wearing a Mets hat with an oxygen mask strapped to his face. They come down the ramp to the side of the front steps. JC is decked out in hospital scrubs and actually looks the part. He's tall, so he has that look of unquestionable authority. Stationed behind the reference desk in the London Public Library, with his shoulder length brownish hair, steely blue eyes and nicely trimmed goatee, he is the go-to librarian for the tough Boolean searches or whatever. I get out and walk around to open the curbside door.

"Did the patient behave himself?" I say.

"Tolerably so," he says.

"He's smaller in person than I pictured."

"That's good. He's easier to lift."

JC takes the mask off Ray's face and grabs him under his shoulders. He also looks older than the picture we got off the Internet. He seems to be sleeping peacefully — he's actually unconscious and should be for another few hours. I grab him under his knees and back up toward the back seat of my Honda Civic. I sit down and draw his lower half in with me, positioning him on the seat behind the passenger seat. We swivel him around so he's sitting upright. While I'm buckling Ray into his seat belt, JC folds up the wheelchair and puts away the mini oxygen tank apparatus. I clamber out of the back seat by the other door.

"Pop the trunk, Watson."

"Shit. Sorry," I say. I fumble with the doors and find the button. My hands are sweating despite the cold. I approach the trunk to see if I can make myself useful. "Did you get his laptop?"

He holds up the gym bag he had slung over his shoulder. "Check."

"BlackBerry?"

"Cell phone. Check."

"He has his wallet with him?"

"Check."

JC doesn't get impatient with me asking these questions, even though we've been over this. While he's packing everything away in the trunk and getting out the things we'll need for the trip, I take a look up and down the sidewalk. Search the faces for questioning looks or recognition. This is exactly the kind of nervous, suspicious behavior I had hoped to avoid. I am supposed to be looking confident and unconcerned, as though I have every reason in the world to be here doing this. I get into the driver's seat to wait instead.

I twist around in my seat to get a good look at our prisoner as JC secures the plastic ties to his wrists and chains his waist to the seat post. Ray is paunchy, slack-jawed and balding. He has small, pinched features and closely set eyes that are slightly off kilter. Friday must be casual day. He is wearing navy Dockers and a blue pinstriped button down. His winter coat is a dark green mountain parka that JC has helpfully zipped up for him. The deck shoes aren't going to be great in the snow.

"Didn't he have any boots?" I say.

"None that I could find," says JC, getting in and closing his door. "Probably has underground parking and doesn't care about the snow."

"So, everything is good?"

"Yes. That was strangely easy. I got by the security desk with our development letter from Ray. I said I was there to meet with him and they told me which floor. I took his pass card out of his pocket, so I was okay on the way out. You were right, the elevator won't work without a pass card."

"Thought so."

"There was nobody in the office. The receptionist was just leaving when I got there with my janitor gear on and I cleaned out her garbage first."

"Fantastic. Was she hot?"

"Pretty much. But it was like I was part of the scenery. Nobody takes much notice of a janitor, I guess."

"I had a little incident with secretarial hotness, too,

but that's a story for another day. Are we good to go?"

"Yeah. You want to get some Taco Bell or something?"

My stomach turns over at the thought. "I don't think I could eat. Grab yourself a granola bar out of the glove compartment."

I get turned around to head west on West 57th Street with rush hour in full swing. Luckily it's a straight shot down West 57th to the West Side Highway and then not far to the Lincoln Tunnel and we're out of here. Just have to be patient like Ray. We were patient with him all those weeks and months when he wasn't returning our e-mails, phone calls and faxes. Now it's his turn to be patient with us.

Just hearing from a syndicate at all was a dream come true for us. Having grown up on *Peanuts* collections, *Garfield, Tintin, Asterix & Obelix* and later switching to *Calvin and Hobbes, Bloom County* and *Doonesbury*, it seemed completely normal that JC's great artwork and my love of word play should bring us together in the art form that we loved. Part of the fun was dreaming up some new concept every couple of years, writing and drawing about 24 or 36 strips and packaging them up with earnest letters to the syndicates, always hoping this one will be the one. Our big break. Albeit a break in a dying medium, as JC likes to remind me.

Everything we sent out garnered us form rejection letters and we moved on to the next idea. We were excited when an editor (a Real Editor!) would hand write a note on our form letter. So to actually get a positive response — and a syndication offer! It was unbelievable. "Pinch me" didn't cover it. Hit me in the face with a shovel, knock me down, dance on my stomach in high heels, this can't be real.

We were e-mailing back and forth for weeks after we got the phone call. There was an endless number of plans and ideas to share: finding a lawyer, settling the contract, plotting our story arcs, designing our website. We had our heads in the clouds and we weren't coming down.

From: "Watson Sinclair" <wsinclair@fullservicebrokers.ca>

To: "JC Dubois" <jcdubois76@yeehaw.ca>

Sent: Wednesday, May 09, 2008 7:06 PM

Subject: Royal Features, baby!

Can you believe this? How many people can say their dreams came true on a Wednesday afternoon with a phone call? This is just the beginning of a long road that will lead us to the Promised Land. All our hard work finally paid off. And can I just say that it is a pleasure to be doing this with my best friend. Thanks for agreeing to take this leap of faith and putting in all that work with no promise of a payoff. That's what got us here and that positive thinking and perseverance is going to help get us to the top.

Anyway, here is how I left it with Ray (I call him Ray, now, you know, Ray Bennett, Editorial Director of Royal Features Syndicate? He's my boy, now. We talk on the phone.) today: he's going to send each of us a package of information on what they do for comic feature launches. He likes our concept but wants to change it just slightly to make it something he can sell to newspaper editors. I know, it's going to feel like we're selling out a bit, but I wasn't married (no pun intended) to the idea of James's profession, anyway. He figures that yoga is huge right now and that making James a yoga instructor will be big with the 20-something demographic that newspaper editors are always trying to target. Yes, I'm going to have to take a yoga class! Somebody tell me where to get my spandex, some crystals and the best patchouli incense on the market. Can you picture it? No, me neither. But I'm open to new experiences if it gets us syndicated!

So we have to think of a new name for the strip, pick a logo, think about reserving a web domain for ourselves and go over the contract once Ray gets it ready. Are you ready for some extra work? Maybe you should take a yoga class, too, just for some visual source material. Don't take any pictures, though. That kind of thing will get you booted out. :) I'll call you this weekend and we can go over all this stuff. But for now, just know that I will not rest until we're in 1000 papers and on our way to number 1 in the strip world. Get ready for *Then Comes Marriage 2.0.* All the best of what it was plus the new stuff we have to put in to make it to the show. Look out world, here we come.

Peace.

Watson

--

JC has a whole file folder with our e-mails printed off in the back seat. I have no idea what he intends to do with them. Maybe he wants Ray to read them all to remind him of how we got here.

"So the chloroform worked well, eh?"

"Yeah. Took about a minute of him flailing around with me holding him from behind and him kind of slapping at my arms and head a bit. And grabbing for the phone and whatnot, but his chair was on wheels so I was able to steer him away from danger until he settled down and then went out."

"And then you changed into your hospital gear..."

"Yeah."

"Where did you store the wheelchair during all this?"

"I just left it by the elevator. Who's going to steal a wheelchair?"

"Good point."

"So I stowed all his stuff in the backpack and then went and got the wheelchair and put him in it. I didn't have room for the janitor uniform, so I put it in his garbage."

"Uh-huh."

"It should be okay."

"I guess. What are they going to do, call Canada and say, 'Got any bearded librarian kidnapper janitors up there who might be harboring a pasty-faced Editorial Director from a doomed artistic endeavor?'"

JC busts out a laugh at that one and it makes me feel better. Talk about pasty-faced, I feel like all the blood has left mine and traveled to my stomach to flush my nerves full of oxygenated anxiety.

There is nothing slower than rush hour traffic when you're trying to flee the country. I sneak a peak in the rear-view mirror at our prisoner just in case he might be struggling with his bonds or pulling a knife out of his loafers or something. Nope. His head is lolling towards the window and he's starting to snore. Please God, may the weather hold. I will never be able to sleep if we have to share a hotel room.

"Why is it," I ask JC. "Whenever you are in a hotel and the TV only gets 12 channels so you end up tuning in some show that you've only ever watched once... you know what I'm saying? Why is it that the show will always be a rerun and it's the exact one you've seen before?"

JC looks over at me, but I keep my eyes on the road. "Is this a script idea?"

"Maybe."

"Can't we just talk about normal stuff?"

"No, this really happened. You know that show with the twin guys who are divorce lawyers and they're both married to ghost whisperers and they sue the estates of dead husbands for psychically harassing their ex-wives?"

"Shut up. That's not a real show."

My wife thinks we're in New York to attend a comic convention, a necessary lie that she readily believed. I feel bad lying to her because she's my best friend and the love of my life, but I don't think she'd support me in this. And good for her, although she's been wrapped up in it from the beginning.

The comic strip idea that started all this came in the most unlikely place: right in front of our noses. As newly married guys, we decided to do a strip about a married couple. Keep it simple, we said. So the great affection I have for my wife's foibles and idiosyncrasies turned into great, funny comic strip ideas. So in a way, it's because of her that I'm here today. Not that it's not going to hold up in court or anything. We'll probably be better to go with an insanity plea, to be honest.

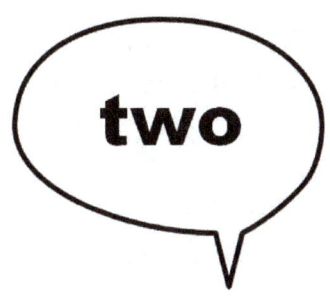

two

We are almost to Syracuse by the time he wakes up. It is 11:26pm on the dash clock. At first, he is just moving around and making smacking sounds with his mouth. But when he goes to wipe his mouth he opens his eyes to see why his hands are stuck together. He sees the plastic ties and sits up and looks around. He sees us and blinks his eyes and looks out the window.

"Who are you guys? Where am I? What's going on?"

"God, I hate your whiny, nasal, superior voice," I say. "Who's superior now, fuck face?"

"Are you with that janitor? What do you want? Do you want money?"

JC turns around. "I was the janitor. Now I'm the jailer. And he's the jester."

"Alliteration," I say, keeping my eyes on the road. "Nice."

"Syracuse 15? We're going to Syracuse?" Ray is just finding out about the chain around his waist, I can see in the rear view mirror. He's looking a little paler now.

"So, listen," says JC, sticking out his hand. "We've never met, but my name is JC Dubois and this is my creative partner, Watson Sinclair."

Ray doesn't move to shake his hand. He just sits there looking at us one at a time and you can see the hamster in his head is turning his wheel. Finally, out he

17

comes with, "You do that strip. The one about marriage?"

"You see that, Watson? He does remember us. We're not as far off his radar as we thought. You've really touched us, man. That was special."

"And you're… kidnapping me?"

"There you go," I say. "That wasn't so hard."

"I can't believe it. You just —"

JC cuts him off. "I can't believe you're surprised. You love demographics so much. Kidnapping is huge with 30-something cartoonists."

"You…" He pulls hard at the chain around his waist. "You both will fry for this! Kidnapping is a federal offense. You'll —"

"That would be true, if we were American," I say. "But we're not. Remember those pesky FedEx bills in the beginning when you sent us packages and acknowledged our existence? They went to Canada. That's Ca-na-da. It's a whole other country."

"Yes," says JC. "Now it becomes an international issue and it will depend on extradition treaties. It will be very messy."

Ray looks from me to JC and then back. "I have such a headache. What was that sweet smelling stuff in the rag?"

Ah, good question. At last he is thinking clearly about everything. This was the part I was most worried about. It was easy enough to find a recipe for making your own chloroform on the Internet, but everybody warned that getting the dosage right was critical because even just a little bit too much would be lethal. We didn't want to kill the heartless motherfucker (much); we just wanted to knock him out for a while. JC was in charge of our research, as is only befitting his expertise in that arena. Of all places to find up-to-the-minute information, we found the best source was the online version of "The Lancet" with articles from 1847. We, like many of the top *chirurgeons* of the day, had been searching for a New Anæsthetic Agent, More Efficient than Sulphuric Ether! It told us exactly how many drops to place in the cone in order to render our patient insensate for a few hours.

The recipe wasn't all that hard, mostly involving buckets and ice cubes. If we were interested in making a pipe bomb or a nuclear reactor, those recipes are there also. We are truly living in a golden age! A golden age in which rapists and sociopaths share information on the many nefarious purposes for chloroform that I shudder to think about. Just as I shudder at the petty dictators of the world with some plutonium, a neutron deflector and Google. We are all in a lot of trouble here.

"That was night-night juice for your traveling convenience," says JC. "We are nothing if not considerate hosts."

"Well, it made my mouth really dry," says Ray. He pops his lips. "Listen. Here's my offer: you drop me at the Buffalo airport right now and we'll call it quits. I keep my mouth shut; you guys get away Scot-free and piss off back up to Canada."

"That seems fair," I say to JC.

"At least he's willing to meet us half way." JC reaches into his coat and pulls out a stun gun. "Here's our offer: you be a good boy and you won't get zapped by Mr. Sparky here."

"Oooh, Ray. That's not a bad offer. He really wants to use that thing, too. It cost us a couple hundred bucks. U.S.! And, as you know, we have no comic strip income flowing in or anything."

"What, you have no guns up in Canada? Jesus."
Ray thinks about it for a minute while looking at the Taser in JC's hands. "I really need to piss. You like the seat kept dry back here?"

I, too, have been thinking about my full bladder for some time, now. This is going to be interesting. I believe that one of those peculiar American rest stops would do the trick, the ones with the picnic table on the sign. There aren't likely to be many picnickers this late at night in winter. We can just write our names in the snow and get back on the road without a problem. Fingers crossed. I search in the semi-darkness of the rear view mirror for Ray's eyes but he's looking out the window.

Now I look at JC, who is a little too enthralled with his new toy. "What do you think?"

"Huh? Oh, sure. You're going to co-operate, aren't you, Ray?"

"Yeah."

I see a sign for a rest stop, which isn't all that surprising, I guess, because they are all over the place. I drift over into the off lane and slow down. The parking lot is empty and unplowed, but there isn't that much snow. I pull to the back of the lot and switch off my lights. There is a little cabin with a "his and hers" and a bunch of picnic tables here and there surrounded by a stand of trees. The sound of tires on wet pavement is intermittent as the late night truck traffic passes on the highway.

We get out and I feel the stiffness in my back due to the hours of driving and it actually feels great to stretch. I pop the trunk and JC heads to the back of the car to unlock Ray's chain. I wander over to the cabin to try the doors.

"They're locked," I call over. JC is emerging from the trunk and Ray is just getting out of the back seat, his hands still bound.

"Do you have any Kleenexes?" says Ray. "I have to have a shit."

"Are you kidding me?" I say. "What are you going to do, squat?"

"Yeah."

"All right. I guess. If you gotta go, you gotta go." I give Ray a few tissues from the glove compartment and watch as he heads over towards the cabin. "Where we can see you."

"I'd like a little privacy. I'll just be behind the corner, here."

"I'd rather not watch this, anyway," says JC quietly. I can see Ray pulling down his pants and then squatting down with his back leaning against the far wall of the cabin. I look at JC and he nods. We both unzip and start pissing into the snow with our backs to the highway, keeping an eye on the cabin.

"So what are we going to do about the Taser?" I say in a whisper.

"I don't know. I guess I'd rather keep it."

"But if they search our car and find it we're in serious trouble. You know the penalty for smuggling undeclared weapons over the border?"

"Is it worse than the one for smuggling kidnapped Editorial Directors?"

"That's just it. If they hold us to talk about the Taser, they'll discover the Ray situation, too." I see Ray standing up to pull up his pants and buckle up, so I guess it is time to get this show on the road. I'm just zipping up and waiting for him to come out from behind the shit shack when I catch some quick movement from the other side instead. "Dude, our prisoner is sprinting for the

Interstate!"

JC looks and then breaks into a full run, zipping up as he goes. I start running across the parking lot, trying to cut off the angle. Ray is lumbering along in the deep snow, kind of hop stepping, but Christ he is moving fast for a chubby guy. There are no cars passing right now on our side, but there is a truck going by on the other side. Luckily there are no lights over here, but I'm sure if someone were really looking they'd see us in the moonlight against the snow. For a second, Ray plunges headfirst into the snow and then he is up again, surging forward. But JC, with his long legs, is faster, especially since there is less snow in the parking lot, which must have been plowed at some point. He leaps into the snow and in a couple of steps he is on him, tackling him by a couple of little shrubs.

By the time I get there, JC is pummeling Ray in the stomach and chest and shouting at him.

"What part of co-operate didn't you understand, fucker? After everything we've done, you think I'm going to just let you fuck off out of here?"

JC is seriously losing it here. I've never seen this kind of rage in him. I grab Ray's arm and try to pull him up, but JC pushes me off and throws him down on the ground. He reaches into his pocket and out comes the Taser, the deterrent I was hoping we wouldn't have to use. He knocks away his flailing bound hands, sticks the black hand piece into Ray's chest and there is an electrical noise and Ray's scream and a weird burning smell that's like no fire I've ever smelled. Ray slumps to the ground, twitching.

JC puts his lips up to Ray's ear, breathing hard, and says, "I told you I'd do it."

He pushes himself up off Ray's chest and walks

away a step or two, taking deep lungfuls of air. I crouch down to look at Ray's face. He is drooling a lot and his eyes are closed but rolling around in there. He convulses again.

I slap his cheek and say his name. No response. I check his neck for a pulse, but how the fuck do you take a pulse? What am I, a paramedic? Or am I, to put it succinctly, an accessory to murder? Come on. Don't die, don't die, don't die. I slap his cheeks lightly with both hands and he rolls over onto his side.

"Ray? Stay with me, now. Move away from the light."

I check to see how JC is doing. He is clenching and unclenching his fists. "Help me get him up." He looks over at me for a second and starts moving. Together, we get him upright and walk him over to the car. He's breathing. Just a little woozy and unsteady. Still drooling — his shirt collar is soaked. In the dark, we chain him to the seat post again and get ready to get back on the highway. Buckling his seatbelt, shuffling around the car automatically, closing the trunk. Nobody talks.

three

"Citizenship?"

"Two Canadians and one American."

"Who's the American?" The customs officer peers into the car, scrutinizing our faces.

"Him in the back." I point over my shoulder. "Ray."

"Where are we all going tonight?"

"London."

"And where have you been?"

"Ray met us in Buffalo and he's coming to stay with me in London."

He ducks his head down to peer at Ray in the back seat. "How long are you planning to stay in Canada, sir?" Ray doesn't move or say anything.

"He's a little drunk right now. He and JC had a few drinks before we got on the road. Typical American — can't hold his booze." I smile at the guy. He doesn't smile back. They learn that in basic training for border guards.

"Wind down the window, sir." He slides open the door of his booth and out he comes and holy shit he's going to go right over there and talk to Ray himself. JC watches him move across the front of the car and smiles at him as he walks by his window. When he gets to the door, he reaches his hand in the window and jostles Ray's shoulder a bit. "Good evening, sir. How are you doing tonight?"

Ray's head lolls over to face the window and his eyes flutter open and closed. He groans and belches. I can see from the dude's face that he smells the Wild Turkey wafting out at him. I can smell it from here. He looks over at me.

"Do you have any I.D. for this gentleman?"

"Yes, here's the driver's license." I pass the license across to Ray's window and he has a look at it.

"He doesn't have a passport?"

"He didn't bring one."

"Well, you tell him when he wakes up that as of June of 2009 he will need a passport to make a land crossing into Canada."

"I'll tell him."

"How long is he planning to stay in Canada?"

"Just the rest of the weekend. He'll be back to work on Monday. He's flying out of Buffalo on Jet Blue Sunday night. I'll be dropping him off."

"Uh-huh." He knocks on JC's window and I roll it down for him. "You're heading to London, too?"

"Yeah," says JC with a big goofy grin, drawing out the syllable a bit. "That's where I live."

"I.D.?"

JC looks at me. "He's got everything. Except a buzz, because he's driving." He laughs. JC, that is. Not the border dude.

"Uh-huh," he says again. Eloquent in its simplicity.

"Here are our passports," I say. I'm ducking my head down to see him out there and it feels like we're going to be in a little room soon. We're not selling this at all. I pass him the documents out JC's window. He takes them without looking at them.

"Will you pop the trunk, sir?"

"What? Oh, sure." I press the button and wonder if I'll think back on this day every single minute I'm in prison or if it will eventually fade from my memory. JC is resting his head on the back of the seat and staring out the front window. There is no sound back there for a second, then some shuffling noises and then the trunk slams closed. The car bobs up and down a bit. Here he comes. I think his name badge said "Doctor Doom" now that I think of it. He steps back into his little hut and looks at our I.D., then types something into his computer.

"Value of all goods received?" he says without looking at me.

"None."

"Any alcohol or tobacco products coming over?

"No. None."

He hands me the I.D.. "Have a good night."

"Thanks. You, too." And we are out of there. As soon as my window is up, JC relaxes.

"We did it," he says. "We actually did it."

"I thought we were finished when he asked to see in the trunk. Thank God we ditched the Taser stateside. I would have shit my pants if it was back there in the trunk and he was snooping around. He would definitely have smelled that. He didn't even ask about the wheelchair."

"I know! Get off here. I want to get Smiley back in his restraints."

I take the off-ramp for Fort Erie. Road signs show the various kinds of gas, food and lodging available.

"Did you know that about the license thing?" I ask.

"No," says JC. "I never even thought about it. How lucky are we?"

"I can't believe it. My parents used to joke that you could get back into Canada with your library card."

"Smart," says JC. "Have you seen how tight they are on library cards these days?"

We choose an empty parking lot behind what we hope is an empty office building. How ironic it would be if there was some janitor shuffling around in there who looked out the window and called the police on some suspicious characters. Poetic justice. I wait while JC puts the chain back around Ray's waist and secures it to the seat rail behind him. That done, he slams home the trunk and opens the back door to put a new set of plastic ties on Ray's wrists. No response at all from Ray. He just lies there.

Rohypnol, otherwise known as "Roofies," was first marketed as a short-term treatment for insomnia and a pre-anesthetic medication, because it renders its users unconscious. It is illegal in the U.S. and Canada because of its notorious use as a date-rape drug. Again, my partner in research was able to find out a wealth of information for us. It is widely available because it is still legally prescribed and sold in Mexico, Latin America and Europe. One of the benefits of the drug for would-be rapists is anterograde amnesia, which means that their victims don't remember anything that happened to them while they were knocked out. The main benefit to us was that we could slip it in some Gatorade and keep Ray quiet while we crossed the border.

At first we puzzled over how to actually get our hands on some. We considered just hanging around a club and asking likely sources, but the prospect of two square thirty-something guys who can't dance would scream "narc" to any drug pusher. Then I remembered my customer Tony, who is a DJ. I helped him insure his vehicle, a tricked out Honda Civic Si with a $5000 stereo in it. There is a limit in the Ontario auto policy on electronics and modified vehicles, so you have to be careful about how and where you seek coverage. It was a low rider with mesh grills, LED taillights, fog lights and big ass tires and rims. All after market parts are excluded or limited by the policy, unless you agree to certain endorsements with the insurance company up front—of course, these cost extra, don't cover it all and require a car alarm. But he was happy to pay it to protect his baby. Well, maybe not *happy* happy. We are talking about insurance.

Tony gave me the name of a friend of a friend, who I phoned, mentioning Tony's name. He gave me another guy to call. I ended up meeting "Tyler" at Tim Horton's and gave him a copy of the Sports Illustrated swimsuit edition with cash in it. We talked for an uncomfortable minute about NCAA hoops and then he got up and left, leaving behind a newspaper with a few tablets in bubble sheets. I really thought I would end up at a rave, fighting my way through drunken idiots lunging every which way. Timmie's was a much better option. But then, isn't it always?

"Watson?"

"Yeah?"

"We're good to go. You going to sit there and contemplate life or what?"

"I'm tired, dude. It's 2:00 in the frickin' morning."

"Yeah, but we're almost home. Just two more hours. You want me to drive?"

"Sure, that would be good."

We'd begun our crime spree two days ago. We left London after work on Thursday and drove straight through to Allentown, Pennsylvania — about a seven-hour drive. We checked in at the Super 8 and paid cash, just like in the movies. Between the Internet and the Movie Network, you can learn all you need to know about criminal activity. We both crashed hard and got a pretty good night's sleep, considering.

The next morning we were gone by 8:00, heading for the south end of town and stopping for breakfast at the IHOP. On the way, we crossed over this really cool bridge which we then saw on the cover of a tourist brochure near the entrance of the restaurant. JC grabbed one because that's what he does. While we were waiting for our pancakes, he read out the history of the Albertus L. Meyers Bridge, once the longest and highest concrete bridge in the world. We drank lots of black coffee and he was making all the tourist attractions sound really funny. We were blathering on about this and that and generally pretty hopped up. It felt like this great road trip vibe, like we were actually going to the comic convention and were just excited about it. We avoided the unmentionable subject of the wanton human rights violation we were about to commit.

"Dude, check this out," said JC. "There's a place near here called *Dorney Park and Wildwater Kingdom* and they have this section called *Camp Snoopy*. 'Inspired by the *Peanuts* comic strip, it features 2 acres of rides and attractions.' We have to go there."

"Tell me we can try running up to kick the football," I said. "Or hang around the Pumpkin Patch to wait for the Great Pumpkin?"

"I don't know," he said, turning the card over. "That's all it says. I can't believe that Camp Snoopy doesn't merit its own brochure. Holy cow, they also have a 'Charlie Brown's Steakhouse.' This place is a Comics Mecca."

"You know, I don't see Charlie Brown as a *steak* kind of guy. More like PB&J."

"Definitely."

After we ate a disgusting number of pancakes with four different kinds of syrup, we hit the road, heading directly north from the Parkway Shopping Center and crossing over the 15th Street bridge this time, which wasn't as cool or historic as the other one. Straight up 15th to Liberty and then over to the Agriplex from there. It probably seems weird that I deliberately mapped out a route that included the IHOP, but it was always a place I remembered going with my family when we would travel to the States. It has a nostalgic quality for me. At that moment, the warm nostalgic feeling was turning to a burning acid reflux, but that's just another example of the dynamic tension between nostalgia and reality.

We found a parking spot near the building and got in line for the Allentown Gun Show. There were probably a hundred of us in line waiting to get in, everybody with their hands in their pockets, rocking from foot to foot and blowing out frosty breaths into their hands. Lots of toques and lumber jackets, which made us feel right at home. Lots of military jackets and backpacks with signs advertising guns for sale did not. We probably weren't the only ones here because Tasers are illegal in nearby New York, but not in Pennsylvania. The line moved quickly and soon we were in the main building of the Fairgrounds which was one huge room with rows and rows of tables and a large opening in the back wall which led to another room with even more tables. We paid our admission and learned there were 840 tables in all. Like this was a good thing.

We walked around for a while to get the lay of the land, not to mention the smell, which was a pervasive B.O.

and dirty laundry odor. There was so much to see: booths specializing in clothing, firearms, ammo, military surplus ("milsurp" to those in the know), hunting equipment, sniper supplies and holsters for any and all parts of the body. There was every kind of gun imaginable: handguns, rifles, automatic and semi-automatic; Russian, German, American and Chinese; Smith & Wessons, Colts, Rugers, Mausers, M27s and Remingtons; 22s, 44s, nines, 38 specials and 12-gauges. There was even an NRA booth conveniently available near the entrance for us to join as new members. All of the vendors were armed — heavily armed. So if you were nosing around in their stuff and they gave you the evil eye, you moseyed.

We focused our attention on the stun gun booths, not comparing prices per se, although we weren't above a bargain. Our main comparison point was the vendors themselves. We wanted to find the sleaziest, shadiest-looking dude in a non-chain store booth who might be open to an alternative proposition. Our search led us to "Chuck 'N' Ray's Taser Town." Chuck and Ray were your average unshowered mall ninjas, dressed in all black, "tacticool," assassins-for-hire outfits.

"Are you Chuck or Ray?" I asked the closer one.

"I'm Ray," he said. "That's Chuck Jr. I started up in business with his Dad, but he's laid up with the gout, so Junior's helping me out with the booth."

I looked at Chuck Jr. and then at Ray, trying to detect a difference in age between the two, but couldn't. I tried to picture Chuck Jr. also "laid up with the gout" and could quite easily. Ray was the taller of the two, with bloodshot eyes and a big swollen-looking nose, as if he'd recently been in a fight. Chuck Jr. had a thin face with hawk-like features and a mullet. He had recently been in a fight with acne and acne had won.

"We're looking for a really good stun gun," I said.

"Well, you've come to the right place," said Ray, brightening. "Ours are the best in the whole damn building. You looking for personal security for the wife or to put a man down in a bar fight?"

I looked at JC. "More like the bar fight idea."

Ray nodded. "Good, cause if it was for the wife, I'd say get her some mace or pepper spray. A woman can't operate a Taser without reading the directions or dropping it out of her purse or stunning herself half the time. I'm not sexist, now, that's just the truth. We also run a full line of pepper sprays and maces, by the way."

"Uh-huh," I said. "I'll keep that in mind. We'd ideally like two stun guns, I guess. The strongest zap you've got."

"Okay, now that's what I like to hear. No messing around. They don't go over a million volts but you can get almost there. You want a true Taser, which shoots out your prongs on tiny wires, or you wanna stun gun unit that you have to jab it into a guy?"

"I think a stun gun is okay," I said.

"We've got the King Cobra Stun. That's 900,000 volts of pure power, as used by police forces all over the damn place."

He handed me a black zapper that looked like the handle of a lightsaber, as used by Jedis all over the damn place. I handed it to JC, who checked in the battery compartment for some reason. We must really look like a couple of rubes, here. I turned back to Ray. "I thought I saw a 1.2 million volt unit over at the Chinese booth."

He looked at me with a look of pure disgust and turned his head to hack and spit a loogie into the trash.

"Them Chinese units ain't worth shit, for starters. Cheap pieces of crap will probably fall apart in your hands in a bar fight. And all they're doing is putting two 600's in the one unit and calling it 1.2. Hell, I've got those, too. But I'm not going to tell you it's anything but 600 in two different places. You're much better off with the 900." He folded his arms, daring me to contradict him.

"Good, okay. Thanks, I'm learning something here. That's why we came to the experts."

"You're damn right you did," he said, looking slightly less miffed, but still casting a dark look in the direction of the Chinese booth. "Plus which, your King Cobra model was made right here in America, by decent, honest Americans. You don't want to go supporting them communist models, because all you're doing is putting money in the pockets of the enemy."

"Good point," I said. I looked over at JC to see how he was coming along with the lightsaber. He looked up and nodded his head judiciously, as though he actually knew what he was looking at. "All right, then. These look good. How much are they?"

"If you're going to buy two," said Ray. "I can let you have them for $100 a piece. Normally they run $120."

This was about double the price we saw on the Internet, but no matter. "That sounds fine, Ray. A good deal, for sure. But how about we say we give you the $120 for each, plus an extra $60—$300 cash," I say, leaning in close to speak in more muted tones. "And we forget about the background check? Can we work out something like that?"

Ray looked at me for a second and rubbed his chin with the back of his hand. "A background check is a very serious thing and it's the law. I can get in a hell of a lot of trouble if I don't do them. But I don't have any worries about you boys, now do I? I'll tell you what. I'm going to take a break in about five minutes. I might see you in the side parking lot near the pole marked C4. Just like the explosive. And if you have $350 cash in your hand, I'll hand you a bag, no questions asked. Deal?"

"Deal," said JC.

four

"Wake up."

I sit up straight in my seat and find that we are parked in the driveway outside my parents' house in South London. They live in a quiet neighborhood, their house a ranch style unit on a private *cul de sac*. In between the double garage on the right and gabled front windows to the left, two steps led up to a recessed front door with a stained glass insert. I rub my eyes, stretch and look at the clock: 4:12. Late enough that my parents' neighbors are very likely to be in bed and not watching the street and early enough that they're not quite awake, yet. We still have to be quiet. A lot of retired people here with nothing better to do than spy on their neighbors.

JC hands me the keys. "Are you awake, now?"

"Yeah," I say. "Let's do this."

I grab the bags from the trunk and open up the house while JC takes the chains off Ray's midsection. It's pretty quiet, with just a low shushing of cars and trucks coming from Wellington, a few blocks away to the East. There is a humid, damp smell of ice and snow that is like water that has sat around for too long. I come back around to the far side of the car and help JC lift our man up off the back seat and out onto the driveway. Between the two of us we push, drag, fireman carry and prop stumble him into the house and down the stairs to the basement. He groans and burps a few times and his eyelids flicker open and closed. It really feels as though he's drunk.

When we have him lying down on one of the couches, I get out the leg irons we got at the fetish store and we hook them up to Ray's ankles. I had previously cut a hole in the drywall and secured a length of chain to one of the metal support beams which is bolted to the concrete floor. I knew where it was inside the wall because I'd been here when they were doing the work, although I managed to avoid swinging even a single hammer. I padlock the chain to the leg irons — he'll be very secure here. We take a few pictures of Ray and some of us with Ray for future use and then lie him down under a blanket.

The house has a beautiful finished basement with a home theater in the den. Ray's chain will give him access to the couch in the den which is covered in a plastic shower curtain, the bathroom, a bookshelf and, incidentally, to a linen closet which is just outside the door in the foyer. We will bring him food and water. This is his prison.

My parents are probably sleeping right at this minute, but since they are down at their condo in Florida until April, it is unlikely that they will hear us bumping around down here in London, putting things in place.

JC looks at me and then around the room. "Is that everything we need to do tonight?"

"Yes," I say. "I'll take the first shift out here. You take the guest room. Go ahead if you want to use the bathroom first."

"I think I will," he says. "I feel like 8 pounds of tired in a 5 pound box."

He rustles through his duffel bag for his kit and then heads off to the bathroom. I sit on the other couch and take a look at our prisoner. I can hardly believe that we pulled this off. Yes, we did a lot of planning. Yes, we prepared for every contingency. But we actually knocked him out, stuck him in a car, stopped him from escaping, drugged him, shuttled him across the border and chained him to the wall in my parents' basement. Here he is. Snoring again. I take off his shoes and grab a bottle of water from the case under the end table, leaving it by his head for when he wakes up.

I sit back down and just about break my jaw yawning. Despite how tired I am, I have to remember that this is just the beginning.

* * *

"Where am I? What's going on?"

"We already did that one back in Syracuse, Ray. Stay with me."

Ray notices me on the other couch and sits up. "Oh, shit. It's you."

"Yes, it's me. Welcome to Canada."

Ray thinks about this for a second and tries to shake his feet free from whatever's on them. He finds them securely fastened and looks down in horror at the chain leading from his anklets over to the wall. "Oh, holy fuck," he says. He leans over with his hands in the plastic ties and adjusts the pull of the chain so he can move his legs over to sit all the way up. He notes the plastic shower curtain as he takes a look around in apparent disbelief.

"You are chained to the wall, but you have enough chain to get to the bathroom over there, to the bookcase over there and you have the TV here for your entertainment purposes. There's some water on the table there by your elbow."

He looks at the water and nods.

"Do you want some coffee? I'm going to make a pot."

He nods again, reaches for the bottle of water and begins to open it, which is awkward with his hands fastened at the wrist.

"Okay, I'll be right back. Don't go anywhere." I look at his face for some kind of read on what he's thinking, but he's just sitting there, looking like he wants to hurl. I walk over to the stairs. By the time I'm halfway up, I hear the chains clinking and scraping the floor and by the time I'm at the top, I can hear him puking up his guts into the toilet. I'll give him a moment.

I gather the coffee filters and coffee from the cupboard and get that set up, and I pull out the mugs. Styrofoam for Ray, regular mugs for JC and me. No heavy projectiles for him. I poke around in our box of dry goods for some appropriate breakfast fare. We have cereal, pretzels, and cans of soup and beans. There's also some stuff in the freezer. Maybe he'll just want coffee for now, but I'll bring a couple of granola bars just in case. I stuff these in my pocket and wait for the coffee to go through. I think about Ray downstairs, stuck in a strange house, tied up in chains, drugged twice in the last 18 hours, puking into a Canadian toilet, not knowing how long he's going to be stuck here or what his captors want. Now the son of a bitch knows how we felt.

After a certain point in the development process, he just stopped responding. It would have been easier if he'd just said no, it's not going to happen, this stuff is shit. Sorry it didn't work out. But communication just petered out, leaving us in limbo. And that's how our resentment

40

built up. We were getting more and more pissed off, but didn't want to spoil our chances in case he was just busy and about to give us the green light. It was a total lack of respect.

Here we are, the key piece of machinery in the economic engine that employs all these editors, assistants, VPs, salespeople, analysts, newspaper people and even paper boys, if they still exist, and we're treated like dogshit merely because we enjoy doing this. If we had to work in an office and hated our jobs like Ray there, or me back at my office — I'll be honest, insurance is fine but I do it for the money — if we were some other drone in the system, we'd actually get a little respect. But as artists, we are expendable, people think, because there is a whole line-up of wannabes stretching out behind us that are desperate to take over and would probably work for free if they had to.

That's where Ray saw us, just another couple of wannabes out of the 5000 he heard from every year. Nothing to this art thing. Anybody could do it if they took the time. With each unanswered e-mail, we got a little bit angrier and a little bit angrier, but had no outlet for this frustration. So it kept on growing. By the end, it was a kind of defeated, deflated, polite fury.

From: "Watson Sinclair" <wsinclair@fullservicebrokers.ca>
To: "Ray Bennett" <ray.bennett@royalfeatures.com>
Subject: Re: Comic Strip in Development - new scripts for review
Date: Saturday, December 22, 2008 2:57 PM

Attachments: New Scripts Dec 22nd.doc

Hi, Ray. Happy Holidays! I know it is a busy time, so I'm hoping we can talk early in the New Year. I haven't spoken to you since June. Until we can touch base and discuss how the development of the strip is going, I can't do anything else. You have all the material. I called your assistant and she confirmed the package arrived by courier and she put it and the faxed copies on your desk. I really hope all this meets with your approval, because I pushed forward on faith that the whole thing would be to your liking. You have all my contact information. We will wait to hear from you before we do any more work.

Hope to talk to you soon.

Sincerely,
Watson Sinclair (and JC Dubois)

P.S. I have also attached seven more new scripts.

     I pour a cup of the coffee for Ray and one for me and head back downstairs. I see Ray returning to the sofa as I reach the bottom of the stairs. He looks pale and horrified.

     "Cuppa Joe, as requested," I say, putting it next to the couch for him. I sit back down across from him and get out the granola bars. "You can have one of these, if you feel like it."

     "No," he says. "Think I'll wait a bit."

     He is looking around the room, ignoring the coffee. I hear JC rustling around in the other room and so does Ray. He swivels his head to look in that direction. JC comes out of the guest room and walks across the hall to the bathroom.

     "Morning," I call out. No reply. I sip my coffee and smile at Ray. He looks at his coffee again, but it appears that his stomach isn't ready for it. He has a sip of water and JC finally comes out of the bathroom.

     "Hi," he says. He is wearing his doctor shirt and a pair of jeans and his hair is a mess. He rubs his eyes and then yawns and smacks his lips like a rock star after a bender.

"Coffee's upstairs," I say. "Granola bars or cereal in the box."

It's weird playing host in this house I never lived in. My parents moved here after my brother and I moved out. This was their perfect retirement pad. All on one floor if they needed it to be, no yard to mow, smaller place overall and easy to lock up and travel. No pets. Freedom is when the kids leave home, you retire with no mortgage, and the dog dies, as my father is fond of saying. He and his golf buddies work that kind of retired guy mojo.

"So," says Ray. "What's all this about?"

"Let's just wait a second until JC gets back. I know you have lots of questions. We might as well all discuss this together. You need anything?"

"No. I'm good."

"I think you're going to find yourself brutally hungry in about ten minutes. You missed supper last night and you just tossed whatever cookies were remaining from lunch, I'm guessing."

"You heard that."

"Yeah," I say.

JC's footsteps on the stairs give us both a merciful conclusion to this suspense.

"What did I miss?" says JC, sitting down on the couch with me.

"Ray hurled, I made coffee... that's about it."

"Dude," says JC. "What was in your stomach to begin with?"

"That's what I was just saying." I laugh.

Ray looks like he is about to cry. He takes a deep breath and tries again. "What's all this about?"

"You tell us, Ray," says JC. "You must have some

idea."

He looks from JC to me. "Well, it's about your strip, right? It's because I passed on your strip?"

"Wrong," says JC. "Check the record, bubba. You didn't pass on shit. You just turned into the invisible man."

"A black hole where faxes and e-mails are continuously sucked in, but nothing comes back out," I say.

"Did I?" says Ray. "Oh. Sorry about that. I get busy."

"Don't," I say. "Don't do that. You're just going to piss us off."

"What? It's a really hard job. You wouldn't believe the hours I put in."

"Well," says JC. "Now you're going to get a little time off."

"What does that mean?" says Ray. He hasn't touched his coffee.

JC sits forward. "We're going to handle your correspondence and phone calls while you're off sick. You just came down with a case of chronic *aphonia*. Your doctor says you will be off for a few weeks."

"Chronic what?"

"Unexplained laryngitis lasting a week or more. Stress related, so you need to take it easy. You won't be talking to anyone, but you will—we will—be replying to e-mails and picking up voice mails from home."

We both put down our coffee mugs and stand up. Ray looks up at us in alarm as we begin approaching him. JC is stretching his arms out in front of him with his fingers interlocked and his knuckles make a great popping sound.

"What?" says Ray as we get to about a foot in front

of where he is sitting on the couch, both towering above him on either side. I wonder if he thinks of the shower curtain as a bad omen. "What are you doing?"

"We need some information, Ray," says JC.

"We have your laptop and cell phone," I say. "We need your passwords."

Ray looks from me to JC and back.

"So tell us, Ray. Are we going to do this the easy way or the hard way?"

five

"I forgot to check what kind of laundry detergent my parents have."

"Who cares?"

"Well, I know that Tide works harder on blood stains, but isn't as environmentally-friendly as that PC Green brand. Mom probably gets the green kind, but is that going to work? We need those nasty phosphates to kick it for us."

"We could always just burn his clothes."

"True. That would also take care of the evidence."

JC pulls a sweatshirt off the rack and holds it up to me. It's bright red with a NASCAR logo on the front. "He's fatter than you, so this should work for him."

"Do you think he likes NASCAR?"

"He has probably optioned a comic strip property all about it. Anything that Middle American demographic loves, Ray loves."

"Perfect."

I take the sweatshirt from him and put it with the jeans, t-shirts and sweats we already have. "Where are the underwear and socks?"

"They've got to be here somewhere, as disgusting as that sounds."

"I forgot to ask him if he prefers boxers or briefs."

"He's not really in a position to dictate." JC wanders off down the aisle, presumably in search of reasonably priced unmentionables and not, say, a lamp. I follow him past a long rack of really sad-looking sweaters.

"Let's go with boxers, then. That way it will feel more like shorts and less like we're gripping on some dude's used gonchies." An involuntary shudder goes through me at this thought. I've shopped at Goodwill before, but never for clothing, strangely. It was a little unsettling to think who might have owned these clothes before and to further gamble that Goodwill staff hadn't missed washing the items we were touching.

"Here they are," says JC, stopping at a couple of racks of socks and underwear on little hooks.

I watch as he riffles through and selects a few pairs at random. The lack of sleep, hyper vigilance and perpetual dread I've felt since we started are now starting to grind down my ability to concentrate. Add that to the residual adrenaline shock from the violence back at the house and I feel somehow wired and sedated at the same time. I blink a lot more than what feels like normal. How much does a person blink, anyway? I'm going to be a zombie at work Monday.

"Good," says JC. "I think that's everything."

"Good," I say, nodding and blinking. "Are you getting this or am I?"

"I don't care. Have you got any Canadian cash?"

"Oh, good point. Let me check." We both get out our wallets and flip through looking for some familiar colorful bills. "I've got nothing."

"Me, neither," says JC. "Do you think they give U.S. exchange?"

I rub my bruised knuckles and just look towards the front window. I remember he is asking me a question.

"God, I'm tired," he says. "Let's just pay."

We walk up to the cash and I dump my arm loads of stuff onto the counter for the lady to rummage through. I pull out a couple of American twenties and watch her punching up the numbers on the register. It seems to take a long time because she is carefully folding each garment as if this were a Yorkville boutique. We're more the "cram it all in a garbage bag and hurry" type of customer, but I say nothing.

"That will be $63.28," says Lorraine, who is also looking tired and fretful this morning. She has on a baby-blue frock over a white turtleneck with some acid-washed jeans and her lost eighties big hairstyle looks a little slept on.

"Do you offer American exchange?" I say.

"At par," she says. She cranes her head to look to the back of the store, as if the old woman picking through the romance section might be a shoplifter. To look at her, she doesn't seem the criminal type, but then again, do we?

"Well, that's generous," I say. I dig in my wallet for my last five and turn to JC. "I'm twenty bucks short."

He pulls out his wallet and hands over two tens. "Here," he says.

Lorraine finishes ringing up our transaction and hands me my change. JC gathers the bags as I pocket my change and we shuffle towards the front door. The pitiful amount of sunshine is still extremely bright on the snow as we make our way through the parking lot. We load up and roll out of there, anxious to get back to the dungeon to check on our prisoner.

During the short drive we try out this laryngitis for ourselves, too tired to talk and probably both thinking that Ray will have escaped by the time we get back and is right now calling the police from a neighbor's kitchen, telling them all about his ordeal and having some hot cocoa. Or maybe that's only me thinking that. We pull into the driveway and hurry inside. I take a moment at the top of the stairs to listen for any noises coming from downstairs, but all is quiet. JC is already halfway down the steps, so I follow him.

Ray is sitting on the couch with his feet up, watching MSNBC on mute. Probably looking to see if news of his kidnapping is rolling by on the ticker. No such luck for him. He has cleaned off most of the blood from around his nose, but his shirt is stained around the neck and shoulders. He doesn't look up. This is awkward. Usually after a fight, you and the other guy go your separate ways and think evil thoughts about each other. It is not often that you buy him clothes and do his laundry.

"You hungry?" I say to Ray.

He keeps on looking at the TV for a couple of ticks, then he looks at me. His face is a mess, cheeks and lips all swollen, and the sight of it causes my stomach to clench. What kind of person would beat on an unarmed man unprovoked? I am that kind of man now. This thing has changed me. That anger and resentment that built up over time has taken a part of me that was light-hearted before and displaced it. How will I ever be able to write light, funny patter again?

Ray refused us the first time we asked him for the passwords, so JC held him while I punched his face. It hurt my hand and made me feel sick to my stomach, but it also felt really good. That bastard deserved it and it was something I had imagined myself doing for so long that I knew exactly how I wanted to do it. He looked into my eyes as each punch was coming and I hope he saw that I could go all day. I connected with his nose on the third or

50

fourth punch and it started bleeding enthusiastically. The next few punches, my hand came away covered in blood.

"Okay," said Ray. "I'll tell you."

Ray's best chance at freedom was being missed at the office and having people start to look for him, although this was still a long shot. Our best chance at remaining undiscovered was to get his passwords and send an email to his office explaining he wouldn't be in for awhile. He knew this and we knew this, which was a kind of unspoken tension between us.

"My network login is 'rbennett' and my password is 'back to work' with the number 2 in the middle," he said, spraying blood onto the front of his shirt as he wheezed out this information.

"What about your cell phone?" said JC, still holding him under his armpits.

"What about it?"

"We want to be able to pick up your voice mail," JC said. He was the only one with no blood on him so far and he seemed very patient and unhurried.

"It's a check mark: 4, 7, 5, 3."

I went and got him a dark towel from the linen closet and threw it to him. "Stay put and I'll check," I said. JC got up and followed me down the hall to the office, where we had set up Ray's laptop on my dad's desk. We booted up and waited while everything loaded. There were dozens of icons on his desktop, so we looked for one that said "Login from home" or "Network Portal" or something, but nothing jumped out at us. I checked "Start – Control Panel – Network Connections" but again there was nothing.

"What do you use to login from home?" I yelled down the hall.

"It's a bookmark in my web browser," he yelled back. "It's called 'Royal User Portal' or something like that."

I opened up "Internet Explorer" and saw the bookmark right away. When I clicked on it, the page came up to a login screen with the Royal Features name and logo at the top. I typed in the password he had given us and clicked, "Login." The page refreshed with the words "Password Denied" in red under the user name and password boxes, which were now empty. I sighed and my shoulders slumped. I tried it again, but JC was already on his way back down the hall. Of course, it didn't work, so up I got and walked back to the couch. JC wasn't there.

"Now what would make a man lie about a password when he knows we're going to check and come right back?" I said.

Ray was holding the towel up to his mouth, but took it away to speak. "I just wanted a break. I'm not giving it to you."

"Okay, then," I said. "We go again. JC?"

JC came from the direction of my dad's workshop, carrying a pair of tin snips. "Okay, let's do this again," he said.

Ray locked on to the tin snips, watching them as JC got closer and waited for me to get in position. I hadn't anticipated him losing any digits, but I was finding you can't really plan for everything. I got in position behind Ray and hooked my arms under his. His breath smelled worse than Satan's toilet the morning after Curry Buffet Night in Hell.

"No," said JC. "Pin him down on the couch with your knee in his back. All I need is one hand."

I pushed Ray down on the couch, face first into the

shower curtain and then pinned him from behind. Thank
God I covered the couch, because it would be covered in
blood otherwise. My mom would kill me if I got blood on
her couch. His hands were pinned underneath him and he
started wriggling and kicking his legs to keep us away, but
JC managed to drag his hands out to the side and trap the
arms under his own left armpit, holding the tin snips in his
right hand.

"No!" yelled Ray. "No! Unnhhh."

"Now which finger is your favorite and which one
do you not need very much?"

"No!" he yelled again. He was really struggling
now as he felt the cold blades of the tin snips rest against
his fingers.

"Should I just choose, then?" said JC. "Okay, I
think we should punish THE finger, for all those times
you were flipping us the bird. This is our 'fuck-off' to you,
Ray." He gripped Ray's left hand in his and secured the
middle finger between the cutting blades, squeezing it tight
but not cutting, yet. "Are you sure you won't be needing
this finger, Ray? Do you want us to try one more password
first?"

Ray gritted his teeth and pulled hard on his arms,
keeping his eyes closed. I was sitting up on his back,
resting my forearm on the side of his head to keep him
pinned.

"Okay," said JC. "Let's see how you feel after we
do the first one."

"No," said Ray quietly. "Don't. I'll tell you."

We all stopped moving for a moment. JC was
breathing pretty hard, looking away from Ray and me on
the couch. I marveled at his willingness to push it to the
limit. Would he have cut Ray's finger off or was it just a

bluff? I think he would have done it, which frightens me a bit. We have a long way to go with this and I wonder what we'll have to do to get it done. We are both absolutely committed and will do whatever it takes. At that moment on the couch, we all breathed a sigh of relief: the limit was within our comfort range. For now. Ray gave us the password and it worked. We were all in this together.

Ray turns back to MSNBC. "I'm starving," he says.

I go up to get some noodles going for Ray while JC works on the laptop. We have a lot to get accomplished this weekend before we leave Ray alone with his TV and his fetters. Our spouses are expecting us home by dinnertime Sunday. Before we leave, we have to figure out where everything is on the server, who all the key editorial staffers are and let them know Ray will be off due to illness until further notice. The mysterious *aphonia* strikes another helpless victim. And finally, we have to copy all of our finished comic strips into the Royal development site using an FTP server.

When the water comes to a boil, I throw in frozen vegetables and macaroni at the same time and put the lid back on. I put a double-sized can of beans and tomato sauce in the microwave to heat up while the other stuff is boiling. With a little hot sauce, this will hit the spot. Not gourmet, but good enough for a management hostage and two renegade kidnappers. I survey the remains of the food box that we put together and realize that this will only last a few days. We'll have to go grocery shopping Monday or Tuesday. First we're buying clothes and next stocking up on food — having a captive is just like having a really demanding house guest.

The buzzer goes off. I drain the pasta and vegetables and add the beans in tomato sauce and multiple lashings of hot sauce. I separate it into three bowls, one of which is plastic, put them on a tray with three spoons and head downstairs. I walk into the TV room and hand Ray his steaming plastic bowl and spoon. He looks at it, but doesn't say anything as he puts it into his lap. I pass him a spoon, but he's going to have to use both hands because his wrists are bound, which looks awkward. He starts eating without complaint, so I head out into the office where I can hear JC's fingers clacking away on the laptop. I give him a bowl and spoon and have one for myself.

"So what have we got?" I say.

"I found the department directory and sent e-mails to a few people who sounded important and to his assistant. I said he went to emerg today after he lost his voice on Friday night. Doctor told him to stay home, could be due to stress, he has his laptop and will work from home, blah, blah, blah."

"Cool. What about the February launch?"

"Yeah, that's where I'm going. It looks like it is a strip called 'Daily Bread.' It's some kind of religious-themed stock market comic. It's about day traders who pray for good stock picks."

I swallow a large, noodley mouthful. "How topical."

"Yeah, help people connect with the shitty economy, see the humor, but also the faith-based solution! It's got focus group written all over it."

"Really, he makes me sick." I turn to the door and yell down the hall. "You are a sick motherfucker!"

"The art's not bad, but what a mealy-mouthed bunch of crap financial wisdom posing as humor."

"At least I'm not a fucking kidnapper!" we suddenly hear from the other room.

JC turns his head away from the screen and smiles. "That was pretty good."

"Not bad," I say, nodding. I yell back at Ray, "Touché!"

"Well, 'Daily Bread' is about to get bumped until the spring launch."

"It's toast."

"Dude." JC doesn't even give me a look — it was that bad.

"I know. I can do better, but I'm tired right now." I feel bad bumping the other guy, who has probably also dreamed about this his whole life, but it's only for a few months and his strip does suck.

"How does this look?"

JC leans back in the chair so I can see what he's written. It looks good to me. Patiently sets out good reasons why this strip needs a little more time and needs to wait until spring launch. About the great work these two Canadians have been sending him and how they're ready to go right now. JC's an excellent writer for a guy who wants to concentrate on drawing. I wonder again why he ever decided to collaborate with me — was it really my talents as a writer, or was the whole thing just a goof and something fun to do with a friend?

"Looks great," I say. I pat him on the back. "Send it."

"Okay," he says. "Hope I sounded like Ray."

"This should raise an unholy shit storm Monday among the editorial staff. But we'll be here, running the show from afar."

"Yes, we will. For now, let's go change Ray's clothes and then I can get to work on sending our files."

"You get the crowbar and guard the stairs. I'll help

56

him with his clothes." Down the hall we go to our duties. I stop near the couch, where Ray is sitting up, bowl beside him. "Mr. Bennett. Have you finished your lunch?"

Ray looks over at me and nods. One eye is almost swollen shut. *Ay-yi-yi.* "Let's get you cleaned up and into some new clothes," I say. "Would you prefer sweatshirt and jeans or navy sweat suit?"

"I'll take the sweat suit," he says. He stands up unsteadily. I help him over to the washroom and then leave him standing in front of the mirror. I go out to the hall and root around in the bag for a minute and then come back with his outfit. I put the pile on the counter by the sink and then produce the key from my pocket.

"I'm going to take the leg irons off so you can have a shower. If you try to fuck with us, bad things will happen. Sit down." He sits on the floor and I unlock the leg irons and leave them resting on the floor by the bathroom door. "Down." I push his shoulders down until he's lying on the floor and I cut off the plastic ties on his wrists. "When you're finished, knock on the door, lie back down and I will put the restraints back on you. Do you understand?"

"Yeah," he says. Not looking at me. Up at the ceiling in a determined stare.

I close the door and I hear him lock it. I look up the stairs and see JC sitting there with a tire iron and the pepper spray. "You okay there?" I say. "I'm going to go lie down on the couch."

"Go for it," he says. He sits back on the stairs and rests his elbows. "Try not to fall asleep."

Shit! I'm on my way to the TV room when it occurs to me. I turn around and go the other way. Instead of lying on the couch, I sit down in the hallway. I'm resting my back up against the wall and stretching my feet out in front of me. If he got it into his head to sprint for the office and dial 911, I bet he could punch it in before I got there and then they would send an officer to investigate even if we hung up. I choose not to say this out loud in case he hasn't already had this idea. Better safe than sorry. We're going to have to be super careful when he has those leg irons off. I think by tomorrow we should be able to let him go without the wrist ties, but he's going to have to earn that freedom by not trying anything heroic.

By tomorrow I will be back home with my wifey. I hear the water turn on in the bathroom and then the sound of the shower curtain rings sliding along the bar. It'll be hard keeping this secret from her. Have to watch what I say. I need to get some sleep tonight so I'm not catatonic when I get home tomorrow to tell her all about the comic convention. So much work to do before then, preparing the launch, getting the sales kit together by ourselves, communicating with the sales staff and booking them all for the February sales conference, getting Ray's assistant editor to run the show because he can't be there — not to mention laundry. I'd let him do it himself, but the washer and dryer are upstairs.

six

I wake up Sunday morning in the upstairs guest room and roll over to look at the alarm clock. Wow, I slept in. It's after 9:30. Wonder if anyone else is stirring downstairs? I stop in at the kitchen to put on a full pot of coffee before I go downstairs to wake the troops. Lots to do, here, people. Ray's still asleep on the couch. The guest room door is open and there's a light on down the hall in the office, so I leave Ray alone and go to check out what JC's up to.

"Morning," I say.

He looks up from the laptop and nods.

"Whatcha working on?" I walk over and stand behind his chair to look over his shoulder. He doesn't look up.

"Coffee?" he says to the computer.

"Yes, it's coming. I'll even get you a cup." He seems to be busily copying files to somewhere, so I leave him to it. I wander back down the hall to the den, where Ray is emerging from the couch. He scratches his head and gives a big stretch, then nods in my direction. He pulls his leg chain up over the back of the couch so he can give himself enough slack to get to the bathroom, I assume.

"Morning," I say.

"Uh-huh," he says, walking towards the bathroom.

"Coffee?"

"Yep." He closes the door all the way over to where

the chain blocks it and I head upstairs to get everybody some coffee. A lot of grouchy people up in here. Let's hope the magic liquid fixes that.

By the time the machine beeps its readiness, I have two mugs and a styrofoam cup out and some sugar and soy milk for Ray. I put all three on a tray with a couple of bananas and a bag of miniature cinnamon buns... bed and breakfast to the stars. Then back downstairs to my cohorts for the day, an editor and a librarian. If I can get a good day's work out of the two of them I'll be happy. Lots to do and not a lot of time in which to do it.

I stop in to see JC first and he just takes a coffee. I bring all the rest out to the den and sit on the couch opposite Ray. I take a few cinnamon buns for myself and pass him the bag and his coffee. He grunts and takes a sip of his coffee, leaving the open bag on the end table next to him. I have a sip of the scalding black coffee which perks my eyebrows all by itself, but slightly burns the tip of my tongue. I switch to a mini-bun, putting the whole thing in my mouth at once. *Mmm. Chewy sweet.*

"So," I say, still chewing. "How'd you sleep?"

"Meh," he says. He sets his coffee down and takes a cinnamon bun. The livid bruises and swelling around his face make him look as though he is in round seven of a prize fight and has to get back to the ring once he finishes this pastry confection.

I wash down a mouthful of bun with some coffee. "Awkward," I say. "How's the face today?"

He looks at me sharply for a second. Then he takes up his coffee in both hands and takes a sip. It would be a very effete-looking move without the wrist restraints. Then he returns to the very direct stare. "How do I get out of here?" he says.

Ah. Of course, the obvious question. JC and I talked long and hard about this. Because unless you're willing to murder your kidnappee and dump the body, how do you deal with a victim of a crime who can identify you to the police? We aren't willing to kill him. We're not killers. Kidnapping and pummeling is where we draw the line — it's a kind of moral code with us. But we also don't want to go to jail, so we have a back-up plan involving blackmail. Also part of the moral code. We're good people, what can I say?

"You help us with this launch," I say to Ray. "And we will get you back to New York in one piece. You can go back to the office, take credit for an incredible new comic strip out there with a ton of newspapers and get on with your life. As far as anyone knows you were just under the weather for a few weeks and worked from home."

Ray is looking at me and thinking this over. He nods his head, but then his brow wrinkles with concern. C'mon, get there, editor boy. I know you're not going to just buy that. "But," he says finally. "What's to stop me from just turning you guys in?"

"We took some extra precautions while you were indisposed the first night. Some suggestive poses, backed up with some compromising e-mails we'll send to ourselves from your computer in case we need to use them. We have the e-mail addresses of everyone at Royal, most of the newspaper editors you deal with and almost everyone at the NCS, including the last ten *Reuben* award winners. You will be outed to the entire comics community."

"What kind of suggestive poses?" he says, wincing.

"The kind where you have a dick in your mouth."

"Eww." He shudders and takes a drink of his coffee,

then swallows and shakes his head. "Whose dick?"

"Oh, look who's Mister Curious all of a sudden!" I say, getting my flame on a little bit, even though that's kind of homophobic.

"I don't know which to hope for."

"Bitch," I say. Actually, a little homophobia in Ray is what we're counting on. JC and I shared a little homophobic moment trying to decide whose dick to use for the photo. In the end, we each did a couple so it was even Steven. Nothing we hadn't seen before at the gym and all that. How 'bout those Raptors? Think they'll make the playoffs this year? No, open his mouth more and shift sideways so you're not blocking the light. I really hope we don't have to use those pictures.

"Let me see one," he says.

Of course he asks me that. "Just a second," I say. I walk down the hall to the office and fetch the camera. JC looks up when I pick it up off the desk and looks at me for an explanation. "He wants to see the incriminating evidence. Our little insurance policy from the other night."

"Which one are you going to show him?" says JC.

"What do you care?"

"I don't know. Don't tell me."

"Okay," I say and return to the den. I switch on the camera and flip through the pictures we took and come to a stop on one that shows Ray's face really well. "Here you go. And keep in mind that we've already downloaded these onto the computer."

Ray takes the camera from me and looks at the picture. He winces and holds it closer to his face. "Which of you is this?"

"What do you care?" I say.

"Is that all you've got?"

"How do you know it's me? And listen, you try to summon up some wood after a ten hour drive on no sleep, dragging a guy into a freezing cold house and taking pictures of your dick with no women around."

"Uh-huh," he says. "So I guess it's yours."

"Never mind whose it is. You can tell who you are and so could all your friends, clients and colleagues."

"All right, then," says Ray. He hands me back the camera. "Let's get started. Get the tall guy in here and let's have a meeting."

"JC!" I yell. "We've got some signs of life in here."

"Coming," he yells back. While we're waiting for JC to get his butt in here, Ray and I are kind of sizing each other up while finishing our coffees. I'm wondering if he really will be cowed by the prospect of the gay shaming. He's probably wondering if we'll actually set him free after the launch. We all have skin in the game here, which is good. Finally, JC wanders in carrying the laptop and sits next to me on the sofa. "Ray, so glad you finally joined us."

"Yeah, well, it's going out with my name on it," says Ray. "Might as well make it the best it can be."

"Oh, sweetie," I say. "I'm touched. You're the best editor we've ever had."

"I know, and the only one, right?"

"No, don't forget the web offer we got from your fearless competitors," says JC.

"Yes," I say. "The one we should've taken. Then we could've avoided all this unpleasantness." I lean over and peer at JC's screen to see what he's working on. E-mails.

"You guys would be in never-ending development hell on that crummy website with no chance of income in sight. Even though it didn't work out, your odds were better going with me."

"I love how you're so sure of yourself, even locked in some basement," says JC. "Always loyal to the Royal."

Ray frowns and waves this away. "Ray Bennett is Royal Features, and vice-versa. I put my heart and soul into that place for the last 20 years. Every launch, every classic strip with new creators, every success and failure was mine."

"Nice to have an ego," I say. "Never mind the writers and artists who had a hand in things."

"I have ultimate respect for the artists and writers I work with. I'm their strongest advocate and I think I help them achieve their best work."

JC snorts. "Does that happen telepathically? Because it sure didn't happen by phone, fax or e-mail."

"I dropped the ball with you guys. I admit it. Part of it was me, part of it was the concept."

"It was your concept!" says JC. He laughs in a not funny way. I can feel the red moving up my neck towards my ears.

"Yeah, I know," says Ray. "Unfortunately, yoga tanked back when we were still working on the contract. I didn't really know until a couple of months into the development. The same—"

"Don't you think that would've been a good thing for me to know while I was working away writing goddamn yoga strips for no good reason?" I can't believe what I'm hearing. I'd like to bust him another one in the nose, get that nice spray of blood going again.

"Yeah," says Ray, totally calm about it. "Sorry about that. I was a shit for leaving you hanging."

"And look where it got you," says JC. His gesture encompasses the basement, the chains, the black eye— everything. Good gesture.

Ray nods and sighs. "Instant karma. So, as I was saying. The same thing happened back in the 90's. I had a whole strip ready for launch featuring a Billy Blanks character and then the recession hit and the bottom fell out of the Tae Bo market. We were this close to cashing in."

"So what happened to yoga?" I say. "The classes are still going on at my gym."

"It's all pilates now. Pilates rhymes with 'lattés' and makes people think of designer coffee. It's cooler."

"Let's just change it to pilates, then," I say. "What's the difference?"

Ray looks at me for a second as if unsure of what I just said. He looks over at JC, back at me and then up at the ceiling for a second, drumming his fingers on the back of the couch. It feels like Final Jeopardy. "Yeah," he says at last. "Let's do it. It's your best shot."

I look at JC. "No, really. What's the difference? Tighter outfits?"

JC laughs at this. "Let me Google it." He keeps on tapping away on the keyboard.

"For me," says Ray. "The difference is that pilates is just an exercise system, but yoga implies a whole way of life, state of mind, that kind of thing. And it had funnier possibilities for you because of the hippy, vegetarian angle."

"I can see that angle," I say. "That's what I was working on with it being part of the couple's lives."

"Can I see them?" says Ray.

"I'm sorry," I say. "What?" I sit forward on the couch a bit so I am fully concentrating on what he is about to say, because I think I know what it is.

"Can I see your scripts?" And here he is definitely asking for a punch in the nose.

"Are you telling me that you haven't read any of the shit I've been sending you for the last six months? Is that it?"

He shrugs. "I already apologized. Yes, I'm telling you I haven't looked at any of it. Yoga had tanked. It didn't seem worth it."

I turn to JC. "I'm going to go up and get another coffee. I'm going to hum a happy tune and hope that when I come back down here, I don't want to punch him as much as I do right now."

"You go, brother," says JC.

I get up and give Ray the death stare on the way by, but he doesn't seem fazed by it. I guess if you repeatedly drug and torture a person while taking him to a foreign country and chaining him to a wall, he reaches a point where there are no new surprises that hold much suspense for him. *Damn it, why didn't we save something good for a moment like this?* I punch the door instead and take the stairs two at a time, saying, "Fucker, fucker, fucker, fucker," as I go up. I'm actually four years old, it turns out. It explains a lot.

After I refresh my coffee, I stop in at the office downstairs to get the scripts and then bring them in to the den for Ray to finally read. "Here they are," I say. I drop the stack of paper with the fax cover sheet that I sent him just before Christmas on to the couch beside him and return to my spot on the opposite couch with JC.

"Thanks," says Ray through a mouthful of banana.

"Don't mention it. I shouldn't have bothered sending everything to New York all the time, it was quicker to bring you here."

"I should be flattered," says Ray. "I've never had anybody go to such lengths to get me to read their stuff before."

JC laughs at that one and I swear I'm not feeling the loyalty right now. "Har, har," I say.

"Okay," says Ray. He has to put down the banana to pick up the package of scripts and put it in his lap. He opens it to the first page and then picks up his coffee two handed and balances it on top of the stack of papers. "Everything's harder with your wrists bound."

I look at JC and catch his eye. He raises his eyebrows, which I take to mean he is thinking the same thing, so I move forward with what I am thinking. "Listen, Ray. You've been a model pris— I, mean, guest. If you're willing to help us out a bit with the launch and you don't go trying anything stupid, we could take that wrist binding off you."

"Let me check my schedule." He puts down the coffee and starts checking an invisible day book in the air in front of him. "No meetings, no special projects… you're in luck. I have an opening this week to concentrate entirely on your launch."

JC laughs and I get up nodding. "All right, all right. You really missed your calling with the editing, you know. Comedy is your real forte." I round the corner and walk down the hall to get the box cutter from my dad's workbench and then come back.

Ray holds out his hands and looks me in the eye, waiting. "We have more of these if there is any bullshit out of you," I say.

"Scouts Honor," says Ray. No smile. His face is blank, unreadable. I have a moment's hesitation, but shake it off. I slice through the plastic in one cut and Ray's hands are free.

* * *

At 2:30, we remind ourselves to take a break from strip discussions and whatnot to phone our wives. Just JC and I that is, as Ray is long since divorced. That was a useful piece of information he unknowingly divulged to us early on when discussing all our great cartoons about marriage. If he had a wife or girlfriend waiting for him, wondering why he never came home from work on Friday, this whole plan would never have worked.

We told Jessica and Sylvie that we would have our phones off while we were Stateside so we wouldn't have to pay any roaming charges. They bought this fairly easily, as we're both known to our wives as cheap bastards who would squeeze a nickel tight enough to make the beaver fart. Of course, the real reason we told them this was because getting a phone call in the middle of a kidnapping is most inconvenient. "Hi, honey? Yeah, I'm just in the middle of bludgeoning a guy. Can I call you back when I've got him in the trunk? 'Kay. Love you."

So now we have to call them to say we supposedly just crossed the border and will be home in a couple of hours. I, for one, have really missed my little wifey and am looking forward to seeing her.

"Good afternoon, lovely lady," I say when she picks up. "How and where are you?"

"Good and at home," she says. "So how did it go?"

"Unbelievably well. I can barely believe it myself."

"What? What did he say?"

"We managed to get Ray to go for coffee with us and look at the stuff we've been working on and, long story

69

short, he's launching us at the next sales conference."

"Oh, my God! Are you kidding? Don't be kidding."

"No, I'm serious. I can't talk long because I'm driving, but I'll tell you all about it when I get home. We're in the comics business!"

"Oh, honey. That is so fantastic! After all your hard work, you deserve this chance. So how many months till the next sales conference?"

"Um, actually, it's a week Monday."

"A... what?"

"Yeah, it turns out he had his doubts about the strip he was going to launch — some Christian thing — so he's going to bump it and put us in its place."

"Wow. That is... huh, and you always said if he would just take the time to look at your stuff he'd love it."

"I know. He totally did. Thank God JC did all those cool logos and rough strips so we look ready to go."

"That's so exciting. But you're going to be really busy, then." She sounds a little bummed about that.

"For sure. But not too busy to spend time with my little honey. No worries, okay?"

"Okay."

"Good. So, I'll let you go for now..."

"Okay. But you have to tell me all about it when you get home."

"I promise."

"Good. Well, see you soon."

"I love you."

"Love you, too."

And so, just like that, the wheels are in motion. Just saying it all out loud makes it sound plausible. Of course, JC has been inking his fists off since November when we hatched this plan, so we are more than ready to move ahead with the strip whenever. Ray was actually very impressed with all that we've done. But we still have a lot of work ahead on these launch packages. Ray and I are writing the copy, but JC has to pencil and ink and color all the graphics and the logos, with some help from a few scrambling minions in the Art Department at Royal, we hope. Should be a lot of fun.

seven

The smell of sweat cooling on my wife's skin after we make love is one of the best smells there is, hands down. I pull the sheet up over us and hold her close so I can breathe her in. All those times when I was scared or worried over the last few days, I missed this feeling right here. I try to imagine the look on her face if I had been caught or arrested, or the looks on my parents' faces. Hurt, confused… disappointed maybe. There were a lot of great reasons for not doing what we did, but just the thought of Ray cooling his heels in my parents' basement and the entire editorial staff of Royal Features waking up to a new February launch feature tomorrow fills me with giddiness and satisfaction. It was the rage that had bullied the fear and caution into a box and then sat on the lid. After I worked out some of that rage on Ray's face, it went into a cocoon, and now, safe and sound and spent, elation is the butterfly that has emerged—still kinda sticky and unsure of these new wings.

"I still can't believe it," says my Jessica. She rolls over and props herself up on her elbows to look at my face. "It all worked out just like you thought it would. It seemed like such a long shot."

"Yeah," I say. I lie here and I lie and I keep on lying. Why stop now?

"Baby, it's amazing! I'm so happy for you."

"Me, too."

We told our wives we were going to the comic convention to corner Ray Bennett at the Royal Features booth and get some answers from him. The truth is that he wouldn't be caught dead at an event like that where the fanboys could have a piece of him. There were a couple of junior staffers from the marketing department, one of whom wasn't bad looking, which helps a lot at an event like that, and a couple of random comic strip artists. We actually didn't stop in at their booth in case one of them was later asked to pick us out of a lineup.

With our new stun guns in our pockets, we left the Allentown Gun Show and drove east on I78 towards Manhattan. We emerged from the Holland Tunnel about 12:30 and headed north on the West Side Highway towards the Javits Center, 700,000 square feet of comics nirvana. The Javits is a beautiful metal frame and glass facility overlooking the Hudson River, with four floors of convention space. There were meeting rooms and the IGN Theater on the first level, the Galleria on the fourth floor and the main focus of everyone's attention on the third: the exhibit floor. All the toy, comic, movie, manga, gaming, book, costume, art, TV and sci-fi companies you could think of had booths and over in Artist Alley, everybody's favorite artists were signing autographs around the clock. The New York Comic Convention was one of the biggest and we had always wanted to go. We didn't stay long.

We paid our entrance and then headed up to the third floor, just flew around the many booths, grabbed some flyers and promos, gawked at all the hot girls, got a couple of autographs from people we had never heard of, took our programs and left. We really only wanted to prove that we'd been there, but honestly I don't know how you'd see everything if you didn't travel as fast as we had.

The place was huge and I couldn't believe the talent: Grant Morrison, Terry Moore, Art Spiegelman, Joss Whedon, and Dave Gibbons, who was hawking his Watchmen sketchbook. We'll have to go back again someday. Maybe we'll be there as guest artists, signing autographs ourselves. They're going to have to improve that Royal Features booth if they want me sitting there. I'll have to send a couple of e-mails from Ray and get them working on that for next year.

"So, you guys are going to be famous comic strip artists," says Jessica. "This bodes well for my shoe habit." She closes her eyes and sighs as if imagining herself at the DSW Shoe Warehouse, which she probably is. My wife has the most fantastic dark eyes with long lashes and full lips, which make for an incredible smile like the one she's wearing now. Good teeth thanks to braces in adolescence. Very petite nose and ears, making her face very expressive in all the right places. Her dark hair falls to about shoulder length, no curl, but cut at a stylish angle at the back. She has a curvy figure that I find very squeeze-worthy all over with about a medium boob. A couple of good handfuls, which if they were too big for my hands I wouldn't complain, but still ample and I don't share that kind of detail with her anyway.

"In your case," I say. "I think they call it a shoe fetish. But I promise you can take my first checks and spend it all on shoes."

"Yay! I love Royal Features now. Which is weird, right? We spent so many months hating them that it's hard to change that feeling, but checks and shoes will definitely help."

"Yes, they will." I take her hand and draw it up to my mouth for a kiss.

"What happened to your hand?" She sits up to take a better look. "It's all pink and swollen. And your knuckles are all scraped." She looks at me with concern, which just melts me. I love that protectiveness in her.

"It's all JC's fault. No, we just got our wires crossed. He was closing the door for me while I was holding my duffel bag and I saw that the seatbelt was hanging out and when I went to push it in, he slammed the door on me."

"Oh, sweetie. Can we put something on it?"

"No, it's all right now. It hurt like hell when we first got to the convention, though. But getting in touch with Ray and hearing that yes took all the pain out of it."

"So you're going to be busy getting this thing going." She lies back down onto her elbow, letting one arm drape across my chest.

"Yes and no. JC has the real pressure, because I am way ahead of him on script production and he has to get all the finished strips ready now in a short time frame. But we are going to be meeting up a lot to go over this stuff."

"So, I'm not going to see you much?"

"For a while, no."

She looks down at my chest and begins gently pulling on various small hair tufts here and there. "That sounds lonely. Can I help somehow?"

No. Not at all. "Ummm... I can't think how. If I come up with something, I'll let you know. Thanks for the offer."

She looks up from her plucking. "Are we going out for dinner with JC and Sylvie to celebrate?"

"Oh, hell yeah! We definitely should. Definitely." I take her hand and push it flat on my chest. "Stop that. It feels weird."

"Tonight?" she says.

"It's kinda late." I stretch my neck to look at the clock as if I'm considering it. "Let me call JC and check in with him. How about just you and me go out for some dinner?"

"Okay!"

She brightens instantly and claps her hands together like a little kid, kicking her legs on the bed in excitement. I laugh and hug her back down to my chest in a tight squeeze that says, I love you so much. This is a kind of posturing we do at times when we're most happy, as if we have to act out our joy to convey it properly to each other. This girlishness emerges that I don't see at other times and I become indulgent and try to match her giddiness. I entwine my legs in hers and stroke the smooth skin of her lower back, wanting her skin on me from tip to toe. It's strange to feel this comfortable and natural with someone and be contemplating something at least partly artificial in how we relate to each other. One of those strange dualities of marriage that I find so endlessly fascinating.

"Let's go again," she says. I notice that she is really pressing up against me now.

"Again? But you know I like a recovery day."

"I know, but you've done it before." She reaches down and gives me a squeeze in case there's anything developing.

"When?" I say, turning on my side so that I'm less accessible.

"On our honeymoon. Twice in a row."

"I rest my case. That's like the difference between Superman and Clark Kent. Honeymoon sex is superhuman."

After five years of marriage, asking for back to back

sex is a gesture of appreciation more than a truly hopeful request, I think. But maybe "just got a strip" sex is somehow like make-up sex or something and it really engages her womanly drives. I have no doubt *she* could go again and she does a good job of covering her disappointment, as always. Her beautiful dark eyes probe mine as if she is unsure of my answer. This is all part of the play, but also a subtle challenge and assertion of a kind of dominance. Why women evolved as slow-to-heat-up brick ovens that can burn on an on and men evolved as Bic lighters, I'll never understand.

"Where do you want to go for dinner?" I say. Dying for a subject change.

She smiles at the finality. "You choose."

"Well, you know what I'm going to say." I jump up to start getting dressed before she changes her mind.

"That's okay. You're the big man with the comic strip and I don't hate Thai food. I just get tired of it if we eat it too often." She lies back on the pillow and stretches all her limbs in a manner enjoyable to watch, all tense muscles and pointing toes, sucked in breath and taught skin, little fists up behind her head and elbows pointing out and then all of it relaxing at once, letting go with a single whoosh of air from her lungs. A big smile on her face as she gets up to put on some clothes, hunting through the pile on the floor for her bra. She has a great rack and I love to watch her put it away inside the cups. And I mean that in the most sensitive, enlightened, post-feminist way possible. I'm sure even Gloria Steinem's husband told her she had a great rack from time to time.

"Did I mention that you have a great rack?"

"Thank-you. Not great enough, I guess."

"Oh, c'mon. You know I'd love to. But the second

time is like trying to hammer a nail into a tree with a wet fish."

"So, I'm a tree in this scenario? And I can't even give you a woody?"

"Already given and taken, your Hotness." We've had this conversation before, right down to the recycled jokes, I swear. "If anyone could do it, it would be you with your tight little body there. Don't bust my balls."

We're out the door in less than ten minutes, which isn't bad. If we were meeting JC and Sylvie there would have been a lot more primping and preening in front of the mirror. More picking through and discarding outfits and changing multiple times while the minutes tick by. I have to look my best. (Bah-dum-bump.)

I lock the front door and then pop the locks on the Honda for Jess. She drives a white Mazda 3 which her mom sold her when she upgraded her car, but we just take whichever one is last in because our driveway is one lane only with no garage. It's a pain in the winter with all the scraping.

We bought this house four years ago after a year in an apartment together saving our pennies. It is a cozy little back split in White Oaks and it has been a great place to live and learn about the many joys of homeownership. Lawn mowing and driveway shoveling are actually not that bad. Leaky roof and two appliances giving out in the first year were the main downside. We drive to the Ben Than in the south end, which is closer and also nicer than the one downtown. I order the red curry with eggplant, tofu and bamboo shoots, because I love to feel the burn. Jess has the Pad Thai — very mild. I've had every vegetarian item on the menu and they're all fantastic.

Jess is less enthusiastic about Ben Than and Thai

food in general because she hates spice. But we make these little accommodations in life because that's part of marriage. I am a self-appointed expert on this topic, having lasted five years despite my many flaws and now about to have a nationally-syndicated comic strip about marriage. We've been through a lot together, finding space for each other and our new selves, these new roles and new titles we vowed to take on. Nothing prepares you for life with a woman except diving right in and taking notes. I've been a slow learner and I've always been secretly preparing myself for the day she'll say she's given up being patient with me.

I think that's why I started doing the strip. I was always so proud when I figured out something new or saw where we weren't coming together on an issue and why. Like it's a puzzle. No, not a puzzle… like a joke that I don't quite get, but I know it would be funny if I wasn't in it. And not the kind with a punch line. More like one with an absurd twist or reversal of expectations. I always know there's a way out of the hard parts and I can see the funny part of our problems and disagreements even as we're having them. Although one of the things I have learned is not to bring that up while we're in the middle of it. Just write it down later.

"So what does this mean for us?" says Jess after we've ordered.

"Us?" I say.

"Yes. How will this affect our future? Will you be able to quit your job and just write comics?"

"Not for a long time, even if we have a great launch. Because we're splitting the proceeds, it means it will have to be a sideline for a long time."

"So you'll be working two jobs?"

"It won't change much from the way it's been. It will be just like I'm writing in my spare time. The down side of working together is that it's less money; the upside is that it is less of a time commitment."

"But less money."

"Right. For now. We hope that if we stick with it, our sales will increase over time. Then we can sell book collections, have a website, start work on a second strip, etcetera."

"I always pictured it being more money and full time."

"Yes, I know. We did, too."

"Do you get vacation time?"

"Not really, but if I want to take time off, I just work a bit ahead."

"But you'll still always be making those little notes in your notebook wherever we go that make me feel like I just said something stupid."

"Not stupid. Adorable. Witty. Wise, even."

"Uh-huh." She's all pouty.

"I could use a voice recorder. Note to self, wife cute… when annoyed." I speak into my hand as if I have a little hand-held device there and my voice is all, Captain's Log, Star Date 315423.6. "We… touched down, at Ben Than… 1800 hours. Here comes… her Pad… Thai."

She rewards me with a giggle as our food is put in front of us. How would marriages ever survive without humor? Maybe this is why it's consistently rated above penis size in women's estimation. That's why a guy like me, with a huge knob and a rocking Bill Shatner imitation, is such a prize. And I'm easy on the eyes, true dat. My mirrors are all perfectly intact. At times like this, I feel like I deserve her love and affection. And soon I will be a millionaire cartoonist, signing autographs, the whole thing. It's good to be me.

"So how much do you think you'll make?"

Back to reality. "Well, that depends on the launch. It's a weird system. If we're picked up by an average newspaper somewhere in Idaho, they'll pay $11 a week for the daily strip and if they want to run it on Sundays also, it's another $11 a week. So a paper that runs us everyday counts as two sales."

"That's all a newspaper has to pay you for running your syndicated comic strip? Like, $550 a year?"

"I know. It sounds low. But the bigger markets pay extra to black out a certain zone where they also sell their papers. Like the Toronto Star might say they don't want us to sell to the Toronto Sun, the Globe and Mail, but also the London Free Press, where they also make sales. So they pay extra for the exclusive rights to run our strip within a certain area."

"Okay, I like that. How much extra?"

"For them it would be $25 a sale."

"Woo-hoo, big money!"

"This is why we can't quit our day jobs. So, anyway, 20 sales could be worth $500 a week but 40 sales could be $750. It's weird. Then we have to split whatever we make with the syndicate 50/50. But Royal Features gives us a $500 a week guarantee no matter how many newspapers we sell to. That's $26,000 a year or $13,000 each, minimum."

"That's only about $7,000 after tax. Why are you doing this again?"

"Because we love it. And we're thinking long term. You build up a good reputation over time and your client list grows and then you start selling book collections, doing signings, etc."

"Book collections? You're only going to make something like 10% on those and you'll probably split that with the syndicate, too."

"Yeah, yeah... I know. But this is all fine with us. If we didn't love it, we wouldn't do it. But the tricky part is the $500 a week guarantee. If the syndicate only makes 20 or 30 sales, they'll lose money on syndicating us and will probably pull the plug before we get started. Our lawyer told us we need to make about 50 sales in our launch for the syndicate to break even. 75 sales would be a good launch. *Zits* sold to 200 newspapers in their launch, but it was by two well-known cartoonists and it was a demographics dream come true. Same with *For Better or For Worse*: 150 newspapers right off the bat."

"Well, there are lots of married people."

"Yes, and lots of people like yoga, too. That's the whole idea. Oh, and I forgot... we're going with pilates now, instead. We have to rewrite all the yoga strips in the next week."

"Wow, the pressure's really on for this launch, then."

"Yep." Gulp.

New York City Police Crash Investigation Report

17th Precinct

Captain Ted W. Berntsen

167 East 51st Street,

New York, NY, 10022

(212) 826-3211

LOCATION	358 E 55th St at 3rd Avenue
	Park's Lotto and Grocery
Incident	Car hits front of store display
Reporting Officer	PO Alberto Gomez
Date of Report	01/26/2009
Date of Incident	01/23/2009
Case Number	NY17/23012009/3462
Time of Incident	18:30
Victim's Name	Seung Park
Address	312 W 74th St, NY, NY
Phone #	646-414-7623
Witness Name	Deshondra Washington
Address	147 W 142nd St, NY, NY
Phone #	212-234-7398
Infractions or charges to be laid	Leaving the scene of an accident
	Vehicular Property Damage under $5000
	Driving under the influence
Other witnesses	None

SUSPECT	
Name	Unknown
Address	Unknown - Ontario, Canada?
Sex	Male
Race	Caucasian
Complexion	Pale
Age	Mid-30's
DOB	Unknown
Height	6'0"
Weight	175lbs
Eyes	Blue?
Hair	Blonde, Light Brown
Other	Big nose, Bushy eyebrows, messy hair
VEHICLE	
Make	Honda
Model	Civic
Licencse Plate	ARCX 980
Dents/Scrapes	None
Other marks	None

Complainant Park was arranging stock on shelves inside grocery store at 358 East 55th Street when suspect's car exited the roadway and hit display of fruit at front of store. Complainant Park ran to front of store when he heard the noise and saw suspect emerge from car and throw Canadian money on the ground. Complainant Park tried to engage suspect in conversation but suspect got back in vehicle and fled the scene. Witness Washington confirms this account and provides description of vehicle: Silver Honda Civic with Canadian plate ARCX 980. I conducted a survey of the crime scene and found skid marks on sidewalk and complainant Park showed me the broken wooden stalls that he had removed to the rear of the store. I photographed both the skid marks and the broken stalls. I obtained a sworn statement from the Complainant and provided him with the case number.

eight

I stop at Mom and Dad's place on the way to work to make sure our prisoner is comfortable and still secure. I open the front door very quietly and peek my head in to see if I can hear anything, but all is quiet. I close the door behind me, drape my coat over the banister and head down the stairs two at a time to take him by surprise. This would be the time he would jump out at me and clock me with a heavy book or something, so I have to be cautious.

"Ray?" I call out when I reach the bottom. "Up and at 'em, sunshine."

"What?" he says from the general area of the couch. I walk a couple of steps into the hallway and I can see his chain leads to the end of the couch, so I'm okay. He sits up and his head appears, hair sticking up in all directions. He rubs his eyes and yawns. "Shit, what time is it?"

"It's 8:15. You want some coffee?"

"Yeah. Definitely."

"Okay, I'll be right back."

"You got any cream this time?"

"No, I take it black, so I never thought of it."

"Can you get some? If I'm going to be here for awhile, I might as well have my damn coffee the way I like it."

"Don't be grumpy, sugar lips. I can get some creamer today if that will make you happy."

"Okay. Good."

I start making a list in my head of the things I'm going to have to shop for as I walk back up the stairs and start getting the coffee stuff out. I can hear Ray shuffling across to the bathroom and then the stream of his urine hitting the water in the toilet. It's all family here: no privacy. If he's going to be relatively docile, I think we can leave a loaf of bread with some peanut butter and jam and plastic knives down there so he can make himself a sandwich if he's hungry. I'll get mostly microwavable pasta dinners to be quick for JC and me to serve up during the week.

Once the coffee is done, I take two Styrofoam cups downstairs to the Ray zone, drop one off next to his couch and then take a seat on the one opposite. He picks up his coffee and I raise my cup to him. "Cheers."

"Yeah, whatever," he says. He is quite the grumpy looking bastard in his misfit navy blue tracksuit, rumpled hair, three day beard growth and puffy pink and scabbed face. Most of the swelling has gone down and now he just looks a bit bruised and scabby with a bit of sunburn. "So, today's the day everyone sees what you guys have been up to."

"Yep," I say. "This is the big day. That 'Daily Bread' guy will be pissed. But honestly, what were you thinking?"

"That one will sell. The writing is a little soft, but the art is good and it hits the demographic that editors want."

"What demographic? Day traders?"

He leans back with his coffee and gets comfortable. "The Financial Services industry employs about 55 million people in the U.S. alone, most of them in the sweet spot for advertisers: 25-35 year old urbanites with disposable income. You guys laugh at this stuff, but this is how newspaper editors think. As funny as *Dilbert* is, the main reason for his success is that he hits that same demographic dead in the nuts."

"And this is why all the yoga stuff."

"Exactly. Although it isn't as strong a correlation because it will hit so many hippies who ride their bikes to the Civil Liberties office or whatever and they wouldn't think of reading a newspaper."

"So you didn't think it would sell because hippies do yoga?"

"I don't know. But whatever. You guys are going to launch it, and we're doing the pilates thing now, so it will be a good experiment to see if I was wrong. We may learn something here."

"Glad to help." I finish the last of my coffee and stand up to leave. "Well, got to go to work. You've got your granola bars and water there, so that'll have to last until tonight."

"Fine, but can you get me some chips and chocolate? And maybe some pop or something?"

"Yes, I can. Your comfort is our number one concern here at Chez Sinclair." I head for the stairs. "Hope it's a good Oprah and whatnot today."

"Fuck you," he says to my back.

That makes me laugh. "Yeah, yeah. See you later."

After locking up, I jump in the Batmobile and peel out of the driveway like the house is on fire. I'm on two wheels going around the corner and the tires are screeching like a costumed super villain being put away by the dynamic duo. What the hell? Holy bad similes, Robin. And who am I kidding? I'm as quiet as a mouse in a very quiet mouse car when I'm leaving my parents' neighborhood, elsewise the neighbors would likely call the police or something. It's as though my mouse car was a hybrid, because I'm a 25-35 year old urban mouse with a very green sensibility, and the car was in electric mode so there wasn't even any engine noise.

But after I'm clear of the general vicinity, I take it up to speeding ticket range on the short drive to downtown because I'm conscious of my lateness due to the delay. I park my car in the underground and take the elevator to the fourth floor. Full Service Brokers is in a five story, red brick office building which is opposite Victoria Park on Wellington. It's a great view out the window and just far enough from the main drag that there are no homeless people kicking around. As I ride up in the elevator, I'm thinking about our launch package and what to put on the cover of the folder and which strips we're going to include and what pictures of us we should use for the back, so I don't see the boss coming out of his office in time.

"Morning, Watson," he says. "Late again, I see." Donald Gill is a pretty big guy, so he can block the hallway very effectively. About 100 pounds overweight, his big and tall suits always seemed to be one size too small anyway, so pleats are pulling and jackets are stretched open and his ties are too short because he doesn't buy the extra long ones. He has huge glasses with thick, dark frames and thick dark hair which is a mop on top, but short and gray at the back and sides. Not sure where he picked up this style, but he should change barbers.

"Am I?" I say. "But it's Monday. All I wanted to do is stay in bed all day with the blanket over my head like Garfield. That cat wouldn't even have showed up today."

He ignores my joke. "Getting to work late is okay if

you stay late. Leaving early is okay if you arrive early. You only get out of this job what you put into it."

"Absolutely. Couldn't agree more. Let me wake up a bit and then I'll be all over this thing we call insurance. I am a legend. I am a broker god. I will eat Paterson & Sauvé clients for lunch."

"That's what I like to hear. If we could capture just 5% of the clients they ignore and piss off in a year, we'd be rolling in commissions."

"No problem, boss. I'm a cold-calling machine."

He walks away towards the reception desk. Now that he's dreaming of kicking Paterson & Sauvé's butts, he's probably forgotten why he was going there in the first place. They are the big fish in our pond and we, along with all the other smaller brokers in town, feel like they look down their noses at us. They write a lot of heavy duty commercial and a bunch of group programs through their call center with vicious pricing. If we take one of their clients we ring the bell and whoop it up a bit.

They actually tried to recruit me a few years ago. One of the ways they got so big is by doing a lot of producer poaching. I wouldn't want to work in that sweatshop, high-pressure sales environment, though. They probably punch in everyday on some time clock like the sheepdog in the *Wile E. Coyote* cartoon. *Full Service Brokers* may be smaller, but it's a nice place to work and that counts for a lot with me. Plus it would break Don's heart to even think of one of his producers crossing the street to P&S.

Don is a good guy: old-fashioned, opinionated and full of bluster, but a real "let me be your mentor" type who wants the best for all his people. A great guy to work for, while it lasts. His youngest son is in business school right now and I know Don hopes he'll come into the business. If he does, I just might go work for P&S, because that wingnut will have us all dancing on our heads. But it doesn't matter, because by then I will be a full-time cartoonist writer. That will be a great day.

I sit at my desk and begin switching on my electronics and checking my messages.

* * *

At 3:20, I switch off my computer and tell the receptionist I'm going out to measure a house and I head to the grocery store for some new prison rations. The drive is uneventful except for seeing the tightest pair of jeans ever walking across at the light on Wellington. Luckily I am stopped or I might just have another New York moment with the fruit stand. Honestly, that kind of firm flesh needs to be given a bit of breathing room for the safety of the general public. I want to just stare, drool and bite the heel of my palm like Lenny in *Laverne and Shirley*, but those days are over, so I force myself to drive on and find a parking spot in front of Metro.

I buzz through the aisles, grabbing stuff as if I'm shopping for myself. Force of habit makes me take the whole grain pasta frozen entrées, even though they cost a bit more. The same with the organics: frozen veg and fresh fruit like apples, bananas and oranges. Whatever is low maintenance for us and keeps him alive. But for some reason I can't bring myself to buy a bunch of heavily processed crap that is devoid of nutrition. Even though I hate the guy. Weird.

The checkout lady clunks down the bag of apples on her scale with ruthless indifference, as if she doesn't care about bruising at all. Oh, well. Ray will have to work around the bruised bits, not me. I watch as "Cindy" listlessly plonks and shoves my various grocery items into the plastic sacks as if she takes no pleasure in her job whatsoever. She cracks her gum and displays my total on her screen.

"91.53," she says and looks at the clock on the wall above the lottery counter.

"Do you offer financing? Monthly payments? Anything like that?"

"Cash, credit or debit." Nothing.

"Cash, please." I hand her five twenties and she scrapes around in her tray for my change. "Thank-you, Cindy. It has been a distinct pleasure transacting these groceries with you."

"Have a nice day," she says. Her look is flat and unimpressed. She switches cheeks with her gum and begins ringing up the next customer as if I have been summarily dismissed and she doesn't care if I get hit by a car on my way to the parking lot. Is civility such a hardship? Why do people like Cindy lack the energy even to be friendly? It is really deflating to have to interact with her. I can't imagine what it must be like to actually be her. I open the passenger door and put the bags on the seat. Does she harbor some tragic story of a dead or departed shitheel who left her with a baby and some bad credit card debts? Why is it someone like me just gives her a hard time instead of genuinely trying to bring a smile to her face? I am such a bastard.

JC is already there when I arrive. He is off every other Monday when he works the Saturday, even though he took it as vacation this past weekend. He is sitting on the couch with the laptop opposite Ray and they both look up when I walk in.

"How's it going?" I say.

"Good," says JC. "Thanks to the expert help we have working for us."

"Ray?" I say. "You in a helpful mood?"

"Hmm?" he says. "Yes. Go Team Pretzel." He continues poring over a stack of finished comic strips.

"Fantastic. Who's hungry?"

"I'm okay," says JC, returning to his work on the laptop.

"I could eat," says Ray without looking up.

"All right," I say. "I'll go and whip something up and be back in a jiff." Nobody laughs at this or even looks up, so I beat it back up the stairs. Don't want to disturb the hard work vibe going on down there.

As I am passing through the foyer, I pick up the bags of groceries I had set down when I came in and take them to the kitchen. I put a pasta dinner in the microwave and set the timer and continue on with putting the frozen stuff away and some of the canned goods in our box on the counter. I wash the apples and then put a few bananas, oranges and apples in a bag to take downstairs. The apples didn't take too much bruising, which now disappoints me in my bitterness. The microwave dings and goes dark, so I grab his dinner and a plastic fork in one hand and the bag of fruit in the other and head back down into the dungeon.

"Here," I say. I hand him the steaming pasta in the microwavable tray and tear off the plastic dramatically. *"Bon appetit."*

"What's this?" says Ray.

I put the fruit down next to the granola bars and the

94

half case of bottled water. "Dinner."

He pushes the fork around in the dish. "This is just vegetables in here. No meat."

"Well, we're vegetarians," I say as I sit down on the couch with JC again. "We're not going to feed you any meat."

Ray puts the pasta dish down on the end table. "Well, I'm sick of this vegetarian crap. I want some fucking cow meat. Just get me a burger... you don't have to have any of it."

"No. That won't be happening."

"Is this part of the torture? What else can I tell you? You're just going to try to kill me from lack of protein now?"

I sigh and prepare to give the usual speech.

"Let me," says JC, putting a hand on my arm. "There are only three kinds of calories: fat, protein and carbohydrate. So let's take spinach, for instance. Do you think it's high in fat? Does it seem starchy like a potato? No, it's mostly protein."

"Mostly grass, you mean. It's food for cows."

"Think back to the Popeye comic strip. You're familiar with that?"

He rolls his eyes. "Yes, I know the Popeye strip."

"Okay. Now stay with me here. The fat 'Wimpy' character was eating all the burgers and the strong, heroic type was eating the spinach. Get it? It doesn't get much simpler than that."

"Whatever. I'm really going to change the way I eat because of a comic strip. This is cruel and unusual punishment and it's against the Geneva Convention."

"Well," I say. "Take it up with the U.N.. You can eat that or go hungry. I'm okay with either."

"Oh, fuck it," says Ray. He picks up the pasta dish and the plastic fork. "I'm so sick of granola, I'll eat anything." He digs in and has a little of the old death stare to share with me.

"Good," I say. "There's some fruit there for you in that bag, too."

"Thanks," says Ray through a mouthful of food.

I sit down on the couch. "So, what can I do?"

nine

On Tuesday, I work right through till 5:00, partly to please the Donald and partly because I've been letting things slide around here and I can't really afford to have any files blow up on me. When an insurance file goes sideways, the first notice you get is when a claim comes in and some coverage is missing or understated and then people are crying and yelling and adjusters are freaking on you. Bad all around. So I spent the day tidying things up a bit and trying not to daydream about our launch for every minute of the day.

I figure JC will be just finishing work about now, so I text him: *Just finishing. U goin over now?*

I switch off my computer and put my phone on night service while I wait for his reply. *On my way,* he says.

Junk food?

Sure. I'll pick up. C U there.

Cool. Veggie burg for Ray?

Good.

I grab my coat off the back of my door and put it on before texting Jess: *On my way to M&D's. Won't be home for supper. Howz ur day?*

I must have caught her sitting at her desk: *Fine. Why cant u work @ home?*

Why can't I? Good question. *Cause we r spread out all over there. 2 messy.*

What about our show?

Oh, yeah. Okay. That's no problem. Home by 9. C U then. Luv U.

Luv U 2.

The office is quiet and I'm the only one on the elevator on the way down to the underground parking. I look again at my cell phone as if my wife's words were still hanging in the air and only gathered in by my cell phone for safe keeping. Jessica is a peach, but I sense she's getting a little grouchy about the late nights and the time away. She's probably going to work late since I'm not coming home for dinner. She does that sometimes even when I am home for dinner, so it's a safe bet. She's a hard worker and wants to get ahead some day. Right out of university, she started working in marketing and P.R. for a variety of companies and has done really well at it, even if she does get a little work-obsessed sometimes.

The company she works for now mostly does P.R. and event management for the local hospitals and their related charitable foundations. Good job security for her, because London is lousy with hospitals. This means that I attend a lot of hospital functions with her, which is okay when it's open bar. Yes, small talk with doctors can be mind-numbing, but I have gotten a lot of clients that way. When they find out what I do, they invariably want to tell me about their new German automobile and how badly their insurance company is ripping them off on their policy and would I mind taking a look at it for them? Cheap bastards all despite the money they make. But they have nice homes, too, and the whole package churns a nice commission, so who am I to complain?

The elevator doors open and I can feel the cold pushing in from the parking area. I find myself wishing I were actually heading home to dinner with Jess and snuggling up on the couch for the evening. I am missing her and partially resenting this project that's keeping us apart. But we're too busy right now and it won't be much longer. Short term pain for long term gain. When it's all over, I'm going to do nothing but be home for a couple of weeks. Make sure there is a lazy weekend in there. Go out on a date. Have Sunday morning, too cozy to get up, these sheets are so soft, slept late sex.

JC's car is already in my parent's driveway when I get there. He made good time. I open the door and I can already smell the fast food, so I let the wafting grease fumes draw me down the stairs like Bugs Bunny smelling carrot soup and floating all bendy around the corners.

"Watson!" says JC when he sees me. "You're just in time for burgers and fries. Our buddy is way excited about this." Ray is nodding his head and watching JC open the paper Harvey's bag.

"Finally," says Ray. "Some real food. No vegetables."

"Thank God for that," I say. "Who needs vegetables?"

"Ray," says JC, handing over some small packages. "I got you onion rings and fries just in case."

"Good decision, I love 'em both. Did you get Coke?"

"Is Pepsi okay?" says JC. He holds out the familiar blue cup with a straw.

"Is it ever?" says Ray. "But I'll take it."

"I got everything on the burger, so just pick off what you don't want." JC digs in the bag for one of the wax paper wrapped burgers.

"That's fine," says Ray. "Just gimme, gimme. It's been way too long."

JC hands him his burger. "Here you go."

Ray pauses and looks at it for a second. "How did you know this one was mine?"

"I got all three the same," says JC, smiling.

"You mean this is a vegetable burger?"

"Yes, but it's a 'fake meat' one and it's pretty realistic."

Ray's face is all screwed up like a little kid who just found out Hallowe'en is canceled this year. He's holding the wrapped burger out away from himself as if it's radioactive.

"Just try it," I say. I take my burger out of the bag and put my fries on the end table so I can unwrap the burger. I watch Ray considering his options.

"All right," he says. He unwraps one half of the burger and takes a big bite with his eyes closed. I do likewise and watch Ray's face as he chews. He opens his eyes and nods his head a bit as he finishes chewing. "Okay, that wasn't bad. It wouldn't fool me or anything, but it tastes like a burger, at least. The ketchup and mustard is the same, so... not bad."

"Harvey's flame broils them," says JC. "That helps the flavor a lot. This is one of the best veggie burgers going."

Ray takes an onion ring. "At least it's junk food and not more healthy crap. I was starting to get the shakes from lack of sodium."

"No shortage of sodium here," I say.

"No," says JC. He unwraps his burger while munching a few fries, then adds a bite of burger to the mix and chews happily.

"So, what did you get up to today, Ray?" I say.

"I took a nap, read a book, watched some TV. Had some granola. You know, usual kind of stuff."

"Mm-hmm," I mumble through a mouthful of food.

Ray takes a sip of his Pepsi and sits back in the chair, staring into the dark television screen. "I paced around a bit, dragging my chains behind me, which is such a weird thing. It makes me think of Scrooge or the Ancient Mariner or something. Like it's guilt that trails behind me, clanking and clinking. I've had a lot of time to think about this whole thing and I find I'm not entirely blameless. There are probably a lot of cartoonists out there who have dreamed about doing this and never did."

"Damn straight!" I say.

"So let me just say I'm sorry again for the way I treated you guys. Busy or not, that's no kind of way to deal with earnest, creative people. Or anyone." He looks at us again and takes another bite of his burger.

I nod and shrug my shoulders. I look at JC and he's just looking at Ray with a stunned look on his face. He's stopped chewing with a big mouthful of something in there. I see him try to swallow and then reach for his drink to wash it all down. I look back at Ray's chain and where it leads into the hole in the wall and try to swallow myself.

"That's..." begins JC. "Apology accepted."

I nod my agreement.

Ray leans forward to get his box of fries. "So, what are we working on tonight?"

"Sales package," I say. "We want to produce the best one you've ever done. What would that look like?"

"Have you got the examples I sent you?"

"Yes," I say. "They're in the office."

"Go get them and we'll talk about what you want to do."

"Spend lots of money, mostly," says JC.

"Every cartoonist's dream," says Ray, nodding.

I put the last bite of burger in my mouth and crumple the wax paper, putting it back in the empty brown paper bag. I walk down the hall towards the office, stopping in to use the washroom on the way. My Dad's office holds an L-shaped desk in one corner and a couple of filing cabinets, a small bookshelf and some low tables all around the walls, with two rolling desk chairs that can roll around the middle and access everything. Every surface is pretty much covered with our launch stuff right now. JC and I are both keeping our personal laptops here and Ray's is sitting on the desk, connected to the internet so we can communicate with the server at Royal Features.

I locate the original FedEx package Ray sent us way back when which contains the example sales folders that the sales force sends out or gives out to newspaper editors to entice them to choose a comic strip for syndication. They are glossy folders with a big splashy color scene on the cover featuring the main characters from the comic strip. The back cover will sometimes show a picture of the artist with a brief biography or it could just be another funny scene from the strip with no text or it could be an explanation of the strip's concept, with the Royal Features contact information in the lower right hand corner.

Inside each folder are character sheets with pictures of each member of the cast, some more scenes around the borders and a bundle of sample daily strips and some color Sunday strips. An editor probably looks at the whole thing in about three minutes and then makes a decision about whether or not to put the strip in his or her comics section. Talk about the importance of first impressions. It's our one shot with every editor out there, so it has to be as perfect as we can make it.

I gather them all up and take them back out to the

den. Ray and JC are having an argument about which Golden Age strips have jumped the shark, which have become the house guests that wouldn't leave and which are just obnoxiously taking up space. Of course, Ray is defending the Golden Agers because he makes truckloads of money off them without having to pay royalties or commissions. I finish up the rest of my fries and listen to them work it over, back and forth.

Something has changed. It's in the way they're talking to each other. It's more equal now and less acrimonious. Like they're colleagues rather than captor and captive. I'm not sure I'm entirely comfortable with the change. I don't want us losing the upper hand, here. But at the same time, I never expected Ray to say what he said in a million years. It makes me see him differently. Three days of beard growth and a rumpled sweatshirt with an onion ring grease stain on the front. Faded jeans and a takeout cup of Pepsi in one hand like it's the nectar of the fucking gods. Where is the corporate stooge whose office we raided just four short days ago? Okay, not short... they were four of the longest days of my life.

The doorbell rings and they stop talking. JC and Ray are looking at me with their mouths half open. There is something cold inside my chest cavity clutching at my revved-up heart, and I blink, take a deep breath and get moving. I stand up and move towards the stairs.

"Ray, not a sound out of you. I'm going to go see who's there." I stop in the doorway. "Shit, our cars are outside. I have to answer it. JC, you're on him. You clamp a hand over his mouth and don't let him scream or yell no matter what."

JC looks blankly over at Ray, with whom he was just chatting so amiably. This is exactly what I was afraid of when I saw the change happening. "Now, goddamnit!" He gets up awkwardly and walks over to Ray's couch, sitting down beside him and reaching an arm around behind his head to hold a hand over his mouth. Ray looks sideways at me to see what I'm going to do next. I close the double doors to the den and then close the door at the bottom of the stairs, which gives me two sound barriers just in case Ray wriggles free. I lope up the steps two at a time. I'm saying, 'Not the police, not the police' over and over again in my head as I pause to look through the peephole, holding my breath and then letting it all out. It's not the police. It's more of an unofficial Neighborhood Watch. I switch on the porch light and open the door.

"Mrs. Bissell," I say to the small, bundled up woman on the front step. She looks as though she's ready for an Arctic Expedition when she has actually just come across the street. "How are you tonight?"

"Oh, hello, Watson." She cranes her neck to get a look inside the house, so I move to block more of the doorway. "I saw the cars and just wondered if there was a problem."

"Nope, no problem. A friend and I just came over to watch the game on the big screen. Our wives aren't big basketball fans, you know." I force a laugh.

"You've been here a lot lately. I got up in the middle of the night on Saturday to get Norman his medicine and I just happened to look out the window and saw your car."

"Yes," I say. "We've been working on a project. Putting in a lot of hours."

"I'm sure your wives must be missing you terribly." She attempts a laugh, but she is watching my face very closely.

"Oh, for sure. But the project won't take much

longer and then everything will be back to normal. Thanks for stopping by." I start to close the door and give her a little wave.

She leans so she can still see me. "Are you keeping the plants happy?"

"Yep, no problem. The plants are great. Good night." I close the door in her face and turn towards the downstairs. Nosy old bat. I take a deep breath to settle my heartbeat and then back down the stairs I go to relieve the suspense for JC. I stop to listen at the first door and hear nothing, which is good. I open the door and cross over to the double glass door where I see the backs of their two heads above the couch and I open them up and hear them both in fits of giggles. I cross over to the opposite couch and sit down. JC takes his hand away from Ray's mouth and wipes it on his pants, still laughing.

"Really? This was funny?" I say.

"Sorry," says JC. "It's his fault. Who was there?" Ray is looking at him with a grin on his face.

"A neighbor. She saw the cars and wanted to see if there was a problem."

"Oh," says JC. He scooches over a bit on the cushion, but he's not making any moves to come back over to our couch. "Well, that's good."

"I thought it might be the FBI, hot on my trail," says Ray, who is a big fucking goof. And JC, his goof partner in crime busts out into more laughter at this glittering witticism. I just sit staring at the two of them. I'm really not comfortable with this change.

* * *

It's hard not to wave maniacally as first JC and then I pass by Mrs. Bissell's house on our way home. I watch for some movement in the curtains or some sign that she's watching, which I know she must be. I look at all the windows in each house I pass on the cul de sac and it feels like all of them might be hiding potential spies. Why is it so hard for people to mind their own business? Is it a generational thing or just an age thing? I would never think to watch when my neighbors come and go or have lights on or off and it would be about quarter past never before I went and knocked on their door to confront them about it.

Bob FM takes a break from the 80's, 90's or whatever for the news. I look at my dashboard clock and realize that it is 9:30 and I am late for our show. Jessica won't be happy about that. I think of stopping for Cinnabon, but that would only make me later. Better to just be contrite and give extra hugs. I don't know where the time went. I know we started packing up at 8:40, because I looked at my BlackBerry to see if Jess had texted me.

I walk in the door at 9:40 and call down to her while I'm taking off my coat and shoes. "Hi, honey. Sorry I'm late."

There's no answer so I go down to see what's shaking. She looks up at me when I enter the room, but doesn't say anything. I sit down beside her on the couch. Our show is on. "Are you recording this?" I say and she shushes me and waves a hand for me to be quiet. So I put an arm around her shoulders and settle back into the couch and wait for a commercial. I think about all the work we did tonight and how much is still to be done. Just keeping up with Ray's e-mails is challenging. There were a bunch from Gerald Spooner, Ray's assistant. The guy has non-stop questions. It feels like he can't make a move without getting approval from Ray. Show some initiative, man!

A commercial comes on and Jess mutes the TV and looks at me. "No, I'm not recording this. I kept expecting you any minute. You said you'd be home for this."

"Oh, don't worry about it. We lost track of time, I guess. Have you changed the channel since it started?"

"Yes. I've been watching a decorating show during the ads."

On purpose, I think. This way it won't have the whole show in memory. "Oh. Well, that's no problem. I'll catch it on the reruns."

She looks back at the TV. "I'm sure you will."

"So, how was your day?"

"Fine."

"Did you work late?"

"Yes."

The show comes back on, so we return to silence and watch what remains of the show. The talking wasn't that great, anyway. Maybe she'll be in a better mood when the show's over. I try to follow what's going on, but I can't concentrate on what the characters are saying. It seems pointless compared to our impending International Launch into Newspaper Syndication and eventual Comics Superstardom. I find it hard to focus on anything else right now.

When the show is over, Jess turns off the TV and says she is tired and just wants to head up to bed. I'm pretty tired myself, although I consider watching the basketball highlights before I just forget about it and follow her up the stairs. When I reach the bedroom, she's waiting for me, standing by the closet.

"I guess I'll just get my pajamas on, then," she says. She looks like she finds this idea very vexing, but she puts on pajamas every night, so what's the problem?

"What?" I say.

She sighs as if this is the stupidest, most time-wasting question I have ever come up with and starts taking off her clothes. "I waited to show you my work outfit today, because you left for work so early you didn't get to see it, and you haven't even noticed how nice I look."

"Of course I did."

"So you're just keeping it to yourself?"

"No. You look nice."

"Too late. If I have to tell you what to say, it doesn't count."

"Sorry, I should've noticed and said something. I'm just preoccupied with all this launch stuff. You look gorgeous as always." I hang up my pants and put my shirt in the laundry basket. So much to feel bad about. She doesn't even know about all the lies and deception and criminal behavior about which I'm not informing her. It's exhausting always having to think before I talk to remember what version of reality I'm spinning with what person. I go brush my teeth because at least I don't have to say anything with my mouth full of toothbrush.

110

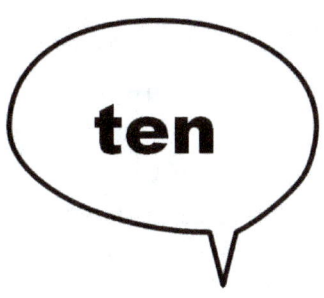

ten

I had a friend in public school who was a natural born comedian and I loved to laugh. I studied him like a rare woodland creature, wondering how he elicited these strange sounds and reactions out of people. What is laughter, I pondered? What is it for? I began what, in retrospect, looks a lot like a study of comedy, although at the time I probably thought of it as no different than the books I was reading or the TV shows I was watching. I listened to tons of comedy albums, the old scratchy needle kind that played at 33 revolutions per minute on my dad's turntable. Steve Martin, Monty Python, Hee Haw, Mel Brooks, the Goon Show — whatever the library had available, I would listen to it, good, bad and awful.

You almost learn more from bad comedy. See what doesn't work and break it down to figure out why it failed. And of course, see what gets the laughs and what kinds of mechanics are at work, what the internal structure of the thing is. I started writing my own comic strips, jokes, stories, dirty notes to pass in class, drivel in my notebooks... anything. Right from the start, however, I was never as good live as I was written, showing that my talent was artificial and studied. But I'm okay with that. I recognize my limitations and always have admiration for those naturally funny people who can make others laugh effortlessly.

I think there is some of that DNA in my gene pool.

My dad is a shit disturber from way back who loves to poke fun and my grandpa on my mom's side was a guy with a love of puns and always a gleam in his eye when he was winding someone up. He loved to quote from Marx Brothers films or Victor Borge's routines and would never be shy about laughing at his own jokes. Another woodland creature for me to study.

I do know that I can't seem to focus on my work on this brutally long hump day that won't hurry up and let me out of here, staring at my computer monitor, trying to focus on a customer screen, but seeing our launch package taking shape in my head. It's really coming along. We sent our electronic proof of the folder artwork to the Art Department yesterday and it should come back today with any corrections or notes for changes. I imagine it will go to print tomorrow, which is very exciting. Tonight we have to send them the final list of strips we want to include in the folders. That's all I can focus on right now.

I decide to go recharge my coffee for something to do. On my way I stop at Beth's desk.

"How's it going?" I say.

"Busy," she says.

"That's weird... isn't February usually a slow month?"

"For new business, yes, but don't forget, I'm working 60 days ahead on renewals, so I'm already into April, which is a busy month. And with all these crazy deals on cars out there, I'm doing a lot of vehicle substitutions, as well as taking calls from clients about 'How much would it cost if I bought this kind of car?'"

"Of course," I say, nodding. "I've had some of those calls."

"How are you doing on the commercial renewals I

left on your desk?"

"Oh, pretty good. Still just reviewing them. Can I get you another coffee?"

"Sure, thanks." She hands me her empty mug and I walk over to the lunchroom, saying some hellos and whatnot on the way as people look up from their work. As I approach the doorway, I see to my great alarm that the boss is in there getting his own coffee, and I hesitate for a moment with two mugs in my hands with an urge to hide or duck into the washroom. Then he sees me. I take a deep breath and press on, resigned to my fate. "Morning, Donald. How goes it?"

"Oh, Watson. Good. I wanted to talk to you."

"Here I am. Talk away." I put down the mugs on the counter and Donald motions me aside and begins pouring for me.

"I've been looking at the commission reports and I'm not seeing much on the new business side for you. Are you doing much quoting?"

"I've been doing a bit, but nothing seems to stick. It's all quoting and no binding, you know what I mean?"

"I know that a producer needs new business like a fish needs water. You can't make a living on renewals alone. Don't fall into that trap. If you just sit on your renewal commissions it will just bleed away to nothing. You need new blood in your book every month." He puts the empty pot back in the coffee maker. "If they don't call you back after you give them a quote, then you call them. Ask them if they liked it, did it meet their needs, what do you have to do to earn their business. Got it?"

"I've got it. That's a great idea, boss man. I'm going to go make some follow-up calls right now." I pop two sugar cubes in Beth's coffee and head to the fridge for the cream. "Thanks for the pep talk."

"That's what I'm here for," he says. "Good luck with those calls."

* * *

JC sits back on the couch and pulls the laptop into his lap with the air of someone who's had enough jack knavery and wants to get down to some real work, as if real work has to involve a Microsoft logo staring at you from one corner of the screen. Ray is flipping through a stack of Sunday strips which are now all in color. JC just finished them all in Photoshop and we printed them out on my dad's printer, pretty much draining his cyan, magenta and yellow. Mental note: get him some refills.

I keep flipping through the pages of daily strips we have been trying to narrow down to the best twelve and they are starting to break down into abstract, meaningless, non-humorous entities. I can't determine which ones are funny and which ones ironic and which ones sweet. They all seem to be melting into an amalgam of all three qualities and nothing more than random images of two people in a relationship seen from some distant window by an ever-staring, voyeuristic eye. Who are these people that allow this microscope into their lives, pimping their joys and sorrows for the possible amusement of strangers? They are me and I can't recognize myself anymore.

Ray chuckles over one of the Pilates strips and puts it on the keeper pile, bringing me back into the moment. His leg chains are tucked in under the couch, so we barely notice they're there anymore. Barely. We could just be three buddies hanging out. Maybe.

"Man," says JC from over on the other couch. "This Gerald guy is a piece of work. Two more e-mails from him today with more questions. I can't tell if he just wants to know what to do or if he's questioning our work."

"Probably both," says Ray. "This will all seem very strange to everybody back at the office. I don't think we've ever pulled a switcheroo this late in the game before. And I'm not there in person, which is weird. And they're probably questioning my sanity for causing them all this stress and work for a strip I've never mentioned before and not vetting it the way I normally do. So Gerald is checking my resolve, I think, but he'll fall in line. He worships me."

"He's not sounding very worshipful, I gotta say," says JC.

"Oh, he's earned a bit of push back and an opinion of his own, but he respects my judgment at the end of the day."

"Okay, good. When will he shut up and get on with it, then?"

"What's he stalling on?"

"Everything. He's quoting surveys and demographicians and previous launch stats. It's like he's trying to convince you that Pilates sucks. Is that a passive aggressive way of opposing the strip?"

"Maybe," says Ray. He thinks for a moment. "It doesn't matter, though. He doesn't have the authority to oppose this by himself. He's probably trying to change my mind in his own respectful way. Don't worry about it. We don't always agree 100% about every strip. Bottom line, it's my call."

"Good," says JC. "I'm gonna shut him down."

"Be my guest," says Ray.

Sensing a pause in their conversation, I say to Ray, "Looks like you've already got four or five keepers there. Are we going to put all of them in the package?"

"No, just the best three. You guys hash it out for whichever you think are the best. I would do two pilates ones and one marriage one."

I pick up Ray's pile of Sundays. "Good enough. What about the dailies? Same ratio?"

"No, your marriage material is really strong, so I would go with 12 relationship and marriage strips and 12 pilates ones. Have you changed all the yoga ones to pilates?"

"JC?" I say.

"Yeah," says JC. "They're all done. There were only two that I had to change the look of a pose or something. The rest just needed dialog changes."

"Cool," I say to JC, then turn to Ray. "You want to look through those next?"

"Sure," says Ray. "Lay them on me."

* * *

"Oh, man," says JC. "This pizza is wicked good."

"Thanks," I say. "But we're so hungry at this point, anything would taste good."

"No," says Ray. "He's right. This is really good. I can't believe this is non-dairy cheese, the way it melts."

"Yes," I say. "Jess and I love this stuff."

"What's it made of?" says Ray.

"What do you care? Plant stuff."

"Maybe I don't want to know. And this vegetarian

116

pepperoni is okay, too."

"Again, thanks. But it's late and we're starving."

"Believe me," says Ray. "Coming from me, that's really saying something."

At about 9:00, JC and Ray and their stomachs were grumbling so much that I went out to the grocery store for some pre-made pizza crusts and some toppings, came back here, put them together and baked for ten minutes at 450 degrees and brought them down with three beers from the upstairs fridge. You never saw such grateful people. We had worked through dinner and finished posting the final 24 dailies and 3 Sundays which would form our launch package for the sales team to take out to the newspapers, so it was worth celebrating.

"Tomorrow we go to print, gentlemen," says Ray. He raised his beer glass. "Great work on this thing. I think we've given it our best shot and now we just wait to see if it'll fly."

"Over 15 million hits on Google for 'Pilates' right now," I say. "It's a lock."

"Let's hope so," says JC and he raises his glass. "Cheers."

Ray and I raise our glasses to him.

"I think you have a shot at a decent launch," says Ray. "With the economy and the fact that you're unknowns, it won't be over 100 papers, but you have a solid shot at 50, maybe 75 if the concept really clicks."

"But you're forgetting the promotional budget," I say. JC looks at me, raising his eyebrow and shaking his head.

"What promotional budget?" says Ray. "We don't do much for new strips."

"Well, this time you've really splashed out in

support of these two newcomers from Canada. And we appreciate it."

Ray closes his eyes. "What did you do?"

I look at JC and he shrugs, so I continue. "We've started with teaser e-mails to all the key accounts as well as trade support ads with a pilates theme that have the tagline, 'There's a man in my pilates class' with the 'Pretzel Logic' logo at the bottom."

"Seriously? Trade ads?" says Ray, his eyes wide open.

"Yep," I say. JC is chuckling. "We've also arranged for a pilates instructor to come in and give the entire sales team a pilates lesson at sales conference on Monday. It goes without saying that we are putting on the full sales blitz, in person calls for key accounts to be followed up by calls from the phone support team."

"That's interesting," says Ray, nodding.

"Yes, and the phone team is e-mailing the launch package in PDF format while they're talking to editors and then going over it with them on the phone. And last but not least, we are giving away a 'Pilates for Beginners' kit to each editor in a town over a half million people."

"Jesus," says Ray. He laughs and takes a sip of his beer. "How much is all that going to cost?"

JC laughs, too. "It's not going to be cheap."

"No," says Ray. "I wouldn't think so. So the sales team is going to drop off the Pilates kits on their visits?"

"We ordered them on the Internet using your credit card," says JC. "They arrived this week. It's one of the things that Gerald sent a questioning e-mail about."

Ray laughs hard at that one. "I'm sure he did. I'm sure they're all sending questioning e-mails wondering what the hell I'm doing."

"Don't worry," I say. "Once the launch sales start rolling in, they'll all know what a genius you are." I sip my beer as if to toast my own idea. I'm loving Ray's surprised reaction and glad the cat's finally out of the bag and we can talk about it.

"I'm sure. But you know what, ads and giveaways are great, but it all comes down to having great content that editors will buy into. If you don't have that, then all these bells and whistles are a waste."

"That is the one thing we've always known we had," I say. "We just need to give ourselves the best shot at getting it out there."

"You know," says Ray. "Your stuff has really grown on me. It's pretty solid. You have such a great handle on the back and forth that happens in a marriage. A good marriage, that is. It gives me a feeling of nostalgia for something I never had. Like the *Invisible Waitress* strip. I love that one. It's sweet and funny. My problem was that the hot waitresses were never invisible. And neither were the strippers, sadly."

"Oooh," I say, wincing. "Strippers are always a hard sell, buddy. Wives don't see the upside there." JC shakes his head in agreement, pursing his lips in condemnation. Or was it commiseration?

"No," says Ray. "They don't. There are so many temptations when you work in the city. All the young guys from the Art Department wanting you to hit the bars with them after working late on deadline. If I ask myself after a long day if I want to go grab a few drinks, have some laughs, or do I want to go home and talk about the relationship? I should probably have gone home more often than I did."

"How long were you married?" says JC.

"Five years," says Ray. He picks up one of the strips like he is expanding on its meaning. "Her job moved and I didn't. But I miss being married. Not the crap parts, like having to answer to someone else for my time or fights and that. But the having someone to come home to, the sharing of problems, the discussion of decisions big and small... the together feeling of shared purpose in life. I miss all that."

"And the sex?" says JC.

We laugh. "That, too," says Ray. "That's funny. That's where the funny comes from in your strip. You just capture the whole feeling of being in a marriage and doing mundane things, like sharing a closet or making dinner together or going out with other couples. Like the one about going to the video store. I love that one. It is such a relatable situation. It always takes forever."

"I know," I say. I point at JC. "This guy's the worst for that. It has to have won three awards and made $100 million domestic box before he'll even look at the cover."

"It depends on the award," says JC. "I like the Golden Globes, but forget about the *Palme D'Or*. Those Europeans will watch any old shit and call it art."

"Speaking of marriage," I say. "I'd better be getting home to mine. Haven't been home much in the past week, if you know what I mean." I stand up and grab my plate and empty beer bottle from the table.

"Yes," says Ray. "You guys get home to your wives. Keep those marriages intact. Learn from my mistakes. I'm going to watch Sports Desk and then go for a walk, I think. Oh, yeah. Not till Monday. I keep forgetting this chain is even there." He grabs his leg chain and gives it a shake.

JC gets up also. "Let's hit one out of the park with this launch and then we'll get you back to the city and all those great strippers and whatnot."

120

"Absolutely," I say.

Ray nods and watches us gather up the launch stuff and laptop, his lopsided grin fading slowly down to nothing.

eleven

"Isn't it weird how orange juice tastes after you brush your teeth? Those are two flavors that really aren't meant to go together," I say. I smack my lips and shiver as if it's the taste in my mouth giving me the willies and not the chill of another uncomfortable breakfast the morning after a fight. She says nothing and doesn't even look up from her newspaper, so I forge ahead, babbling nonsensically. "We did a comic strip about that. Sorry if my material isn't as fresh as this great juice. Where do we get this stuff? Is it from concentrate?"

I haven't been home for dinner any night this week, which is taking its toll. We're going straight from work to the launch station every day to work feverishly on promotional materials, bios, new scripts, character profiles... the list is never ending. Ray has us busting our asses doing stuff we never even considered a part of comic strips or a launch. I really question how we would have pulled this off without his help now, because there is no way the people at the Royal Features office would have bought that our pathetic set of directions were coming from Ray. Who knew that you have to customize your demographics insert sheet by region and by size of market? We have about six different profiles of our target audience, each one showing how we hit it dead center.

It's exciting to be finally working with Ray, because he is a legend in the business and we had always dreamed of someday collaborating with him. Just not like this. But it's playing proper hell with my home life. I wonder if the boys could do without me for a night, so I can make it up to the wife? Jessica is not impressed with being neglected and can't understand why JC and I don't work here in our apartment so she can at least feel a part of the action. This is a hard one to explain, which she is smart enough to figure out and so is choosing to be hurt by it. Of course, the conflict is giving me all sorts of script ideas, which is good in a way.

We've been conditioned by sitcoms on how to behave in a marriage. Married people trade barbs and keep up a steady stream of one-liners and ironic spousal deprecation and the studio audience yuks it up appreciatively. In reality, hurtful comments aren't as funny as they seem on TV and the studio audience tends to feel that the other cast member is just being insensitive. That's why I try to keep most of my witty banter for the strip.

"What about dinner and a movie tonight?" I say. Just floating a first reparation payment offer.

"On a Thursday night?" she says, still not looking up.

"You get to choose the movie."

Now she looks up. "And the restaurant?"

"Yes, both. Just to say sorry for what a crumb bum I've been."

"That's a nicer way of saying what I said."

"All right, I've been an asshole. Can you forgive me?" I reach out for her hand, as they often do in the movies. I try my winningest smile. She smiles a little bit and then jabs her fork into my hand as punishment for breaking down her defenses. "Ouch!"

"Stop trying to get in my good books."

"Oh, I should just give up and stay in the dog house? What's next, sleeping on the couch?"

"Honestly?" She looks as if she's considering it. "I think we're not doing so good. Never mind the last week; at least I know there's a reason for it. But we keep having the same conversations and nothing ever changes. Just the excuses are new. I think next is you moving out for a while. Or for good."

No way I'm touching that. "So what movie do you want to see?" That is some scary shit right there. Of course we have the same conversations, because she keeps bringing up the same problems that I don't know how to fix. Can't she just live with the things that can't change? How am I supposed to know what's a deal breaker and what's a toilet seat or toothpaste cap? The Boss says, 'You've got to learn to live with what you can't rise above.' Amen, brother. I can say that there's a lot of stuff I've had to rise above, too. My wife is a bundle of neuroses wrapped in a shell of contradictions and a hot button temper. But that's her and I love her. Case closed. No doghouse and no difficult conversations.

"What's playing?" she says, giving up and turning to the Entertainment section.

"There has to be some hardcore chick flick going on. One with lots of weeping and grand gestures."

"A romcom with all the trimmings?"

"You know I love Hugh Grant." I actually don't find that romcoms are a good place to get material, because they aren't real. So you end up with an imitation of an imitation. But the situation of us going to romcoms is real and what we talk about is real, and I can translate that into an imitation of what is real and what is really funny. I hope. But overall I don't mind chick flicks. At least there are a few laughs. If only we could see the *Ike & Tina Turner Story* again. That way we get about two weeks of thinking I'm not that bad as husbands go.

One of the first nice things Ray said to me about the strip, back when he was trying to get us to sign a contract, was that the writing felt real. It's almost voyeuristic, he said, because it's like you're eavesdropping on a real marriage. *Yeah*, said Jessica at the time. *My marriage.* But I always feel like a bit of a fraud in that way. James and Stella's relationship in the strip is a kind of idealized version of ours: with warts, with conflict, but without this feeling of inadequacy. Jess is a really good person and I love her for it, but on some ugly, stinking, sweltering, subcutaneous level, this makes me feel worse about myself, which manifests itself in a kind of resentment towards her.

I am conscious of these feelings sometimes, but I'm not a sophisticated enough writer to write about them. The problems in the strip are not the sort of insurmountable, recurring grudge matches we have to keep fighting out. Their problems are the kind that are resolved by patience and understanding, the ones I recognize and have seen us work through. But I guess if the strip were a mirror for reality, I would write a James who doesn't feel worthy of Stella's love. And maybe that's the source of the problems I can't solve.

"Well," I say, getting up and checking the time on my cell phone. "If I was Dagwood Bumstead right now, I'd be pulling my jacket on, grabbing a kiss and my briefcase from you as I run out the door. You know Mr. Dithers will kick my ass if I'm late again."

"Yes," she says. "You better go." She looks steadily at me as I come over to her chair and give her a kiss on the cheek.

"See you tonight."
"Yes."

* * *

The good thing about my office peeps is that they always love me for who I am: a guy who brings in donuts when he wants to feel popular. I left home at a decent hour today, mostly because I wanted to get the hell away from that unresolved tension, and I didn't stop at the launch station. So when I walk in at 8:20 with a box of Tim Horton's assorted, the Donald is standing in his doorway and gives me a happy "Good Morning" as he takes a Boston Cream off my hands. I stop by and offer one to Beth, whose desk is right outside my office, before continuing on to the lunchroom minus one Boston Cream and one Lemon Filled. Got the most important people covered, anyway.

I sit down at my desk and see piles everywhere I look. Beth has left me a bunch of renewals to look over—probably because they've gone up and the clients are bitching. There are a bunch of new quotes to get to whenever I have a moment not spent on Google looking up stuff for the launch. The phone messages will have to wait until I check my e-mail. E-mail is the easiest thing to do, because it's like Ping-Pong. You just bat the ball back to the other guy without having to catch him at his desk or talk for a long time. Once and done. I see one from my Father, so I go there first.

I read his missive with mounting incredulity and then pick up the phone and dial his number.

127

"Hello?"

"Hey, Dad. It's your son, Watson."

"What son?"

"Right, Watson. Calling from London. How are you guys doing down there?"

"Good, son. What's going on?" Instantly suspicious because I never call. My mom will probably be assuming the worst and waiting to hear who died, holding onto my Dad's elbow so she can listen in.

"You guys must be loving it down there with all that sunshine."

"I suppose so."

"It is miserable here. February in Ontario is not the place you want to be right now, that's for sure."

"Do you want to come and visit or something?"

"No, no. Just saying I'm jealous, that's all. So, listen. I got your e-mail about Melissa having her baby. That is such great news! Eight pounds, two ounces... he's going to be a big boy, am I right?"

"Well, look at his father."

"Sure. That guy, whew! But I was thinking about your idea of coming back early to see the baby."

"Yes?"

"Well, they're going to be so busy with all the stuff that goes with being a new parent. Which end the diaper goes on, how to drive a car on two hours sleep... all that stuff. Do you really think they'll want lots of relatives crowding around to see the baby?"

"Huh. But I think they're going to be anxious to show him off."

"And they'll have lots of time for that when they've had a chance to catch their breath. I just think we should wait till the second wave of gawkers and well-wishers. In a month or two."

"Oh."

"That way, you guys get to enjoy some more good weather and we don't feel like we're intruding."

"I see. I suppose so."

"What does Mom say? I can hear her breathing."

"Oh, that must be me. Your mother is out with her Thursday golf group."

"Really? Well, I'm sure she wouldn't want to be a nuisance."

"True. And we would miss a month or so of the golf we've paid for."

"Tell me about it. You want that swing tuned up for your triumphant return to the Highland this spring."

"Is everything okay, Watson?"

"Sure, sure. Just really busy right now."

"How's Jessica? All's well with you guys?"

"Oh, yeah. Jess is great."

"All right. Good talking to you. Let me discuss this with your mother. I think she is pretty eager to go right away, but let's see what she says."

"Great. Give me a call or send me an e-mail when you know your plans."

"Okay, bye. Will do."

"Bye, Dad."

Oh, my God. What kind of a shit show would that be? My parents come home to find a hostage in their basement and the place a disaster. Some caretaker I turned out to be. I'm trying to remember the last time I watered the plants and I still have to drywall over the hole we cut in the wall to secure the chain. I need time. And by the same token, we have got to wrap this thing up as soon as possible after the launch. Get Ray to Buffalo and stick him on a plane for real. The longer it takes the more risky the whole operation.

Turning to the piles of paper on my desk, I decide that I should make some headway there also. I can't bring myself to care too much about the renewals. Some will stay and some will get a price somewhere else and leave me. I move them all to the outgoing mail pile. Ship them out. At least they have coverage. The ones I worry about are the ones where there is no coverage and a deadline is looming. Disaster lurks inside any pile of paper in an insurance office, like the one house or car that doesn't get coverage right before a tornado. Always a nice story for the newspaper when a decent, hardworking single mom thought she had insured her precious belongings and some lazy broker or agent didn't get around to binding her policy.

I'm just not that focused on my customers right now. I'm happy getting the basics done and not too interested in going the extra mile. I'm about to get an infusion of additional income from my cartoonist gig and that's where I need to be concentrating. I bounce a few e-mails back to underwriters with answers to their questions. Looking through the pile of phone messages, I throw out all the requests for quotation from new prospects. No time, no care. My customer Massimo De Luca has bought himself a Lexus and needs a pink slip to pick it up at the dealership by Friday. I can do that.

I print out the slips and a copy of our binder for the dealership, put them in an envelope and leave them at the reception desk for Massimo to pick up tomorrow. Wow, I got something done; I feel light-headed. I think this justifies some more work on the strip launch. I've been twittering to my tweeps about the coming launch and also dropping teasers on the usenet and in the blogosphere, trying to get people talking about it. I've also set up accounts on all the webcomic portals and we've been posting teaser strips this week just to heighten the anticipation before the launch. These will be linked to our Royal Features page and also to our own website. We've already been getting hits and all that's up right now is our bios and character sketches.

I pull up the rec.arts.comics.strips page in Google Reader to post another few comments, but after ten minutes I am still just reading all the posts, catching up with all the eccentrics. And then I click on a few of their blog links and that takes up more time, but at least I make a few comment entries there, too. But then I follow some links and read a few webcomics here and there. The next time I look up from my screen, it is lunchtime and the office is quiet.

I decide to get out of there and swing by the ranch to see what's percolating. I tell the receptionist I have to call on some customers and won't be back for awhile, but the truth is I haven't booked any calls in a long while. I think JC is on a 1:00 to 9:00 today, so he'll probably be over there for a while longer. I beetle over in my little Honda in under ten minutes and pull up beside JC's shaggin' wagon: TDI Jetta. I see the curtains move in the window of Mrs. Bissell's house. She peeks out at me so I wave and she darts back into her living room. The front door is open and I call out as I walk in. "Honey… I'm home. What's for lunch?" I hear them talking downstairs so I ditch my coat and head down there first. They are on opposite couches, both staring at the TV with remote controls in their hands. What's this? JC's PS2 is hooked up and they are playing some kind of racing game.

"Hey, Watson," says Ray. "I'm kicking your buddy's ass here." He looks different with a week's worth of beard growth and his face all healed and back to normal. He's wearing the jeans and NASCAR hoodie that we got him at Goodwill. I swear he has lost weight. I don't think of him as such a corporate pinhead with this slacker look and with all the time we've spent hanging out with him, so it's harder to hate him.

"Like hell you are!" says JC. "You're half a lap ahead, butt munch." JC is dressed for work at the library: Dockers and striped button down with a light sweater.

"I'm going up to get some lunch," I say to no one in particular.

"Okay."

"Okay."

Neither of them looks up as I leave the room and march up to the kitchen all stompy like. I wonder when the hell those two became pals over the last week. That's the first I've seen of the video game system and the thought of them goofing off here all morning doesn't feel too good. Is that because I'm jealous of this buddy-buddy vibe they've got going? Or because I'm pissed they might not have done any work on the strip today? It's not that complicated, idiot. Fuck them. It's both. Time for a little PB&J and sulking. We'll see how long they can stand the heat.

When we were kids, JC tended to be really easy-going about who he was friends with and I didn't like it then, either. I tended to focus on one friend to the exclusion of all others. I was a firm believer in the concept of a "best friend." JC would let other guys go downtown with us if they asked, so we would always end up with some third wheel hanging around when we went to the comic store or played video games. Guys who had never even heard of modeling were all of a sudden tagging along with us to McCormick's Hobby Center to look at the model car kits, planes, spacecraft and military equipment. And just because JC was always the Dungeon Master, he felt free to invite whomever he wanted to play in our Friday night games of D&D, even the dudes who always wanted to make their characters something like a chaotic evil Paladin. Hello? Contradiction!

It did annoy me, but it was always the two of us and some other satellite friend or other, so that was okay. As long as he understood that I was the "best friend," it was only a minor inconvenience to expand our circle of friends to those other dweebs. I felt I had a proprietary interest in JC—that I had "discovered" him and his ability to draw any spacecraft from the Star Wars movies in thrilling detail. That's grounds for minor celebrity status in Fifth Grade. When I started writing up some booger jokes for him to draw into comic strips, that sealed the deal for me. We had each other's backs from then on. We were compadres. Yes, sometimes other schmucks would also want to skip school to stand in line with us all day for tickets to *Back to the Future* on opening day, but that's just a side show to us, the main event.

As if he's in tune with my thoughts at that moment, JC comes wandering into the kitchen to see where I've gone. "Hey, guy. What are you doing up here?"

"Having lunch. What are you doing down there?"

He looks puzzled. "What do you mean?"

"Video games? He's supposed to be our prisoner, not our buddy."

JC leans up against the kitchen counter and crosses his arms. "Dude said he was bored. I thought this might help keep him in a cooperative mood."

"We've got a lot of work to do here. I don't think anyone has time to be fooling around playing video games."

"Chill out, man. You gonna let him work on the laptop while we're not here? Send whatever e-mails he wants? He's alone for, like, ten hours a day."

I pause in acknowledgment of a good point. "I guess so." I take a big mouthful of my sandwich and chew peevishly.

"Anyway, I gotta go," JC says. "I'm due on the info desk at 1:00."

I stand up and follow him into the kitchen, putting my plate by the sink. "Yeah, okay. Are you coming back after 9:00?"

"I don't think so. I got a lot done this morning and Sylvie wants my warm body at home tonight."

"Okay. Can you get anything done at work today?"

He grabs his coat from the front hall closet. "Yeah, I'll do what I can on break or slow times."

"Good. I can't believe the sales conference is next Monday and how much shit we still have to do."

"This is why Ray logs such crazy hours. He doesn't trust this stuff to anyone else so he puts it on himself. That's how he got so run down. Did you know he's been seeing a doctor for depression? He's on meds and everything."

"He told you that?"

"Yeah, we got talking this morning. That dude has a shit life. No girlfriend in over three years. Works eighty, ninety-hour weeks. Eats nothing but junk food."

"Did he get teary... all choked up? Maybe cry on your shoulder a little bit?"

JC opens the front door and turns back to look at me as if trying to figure out who I am. "What's your problem, man?" He zips up his coat.

I move in close to talk in a low voice so Ray can't hear me down at the bottom of the stairs. "That's Ray Bennett down there, okay? The asshole who left us hanging all those months and never read my stuff. The shittier his life is, the happier I am."

"Okay, whatever. Listen, I gotta go." JC walks out onto the front walk towards his car.

"Okay, shit. I'm sorry. I'm not sleeping much and I'm way overworked, that's all."

"Go play a few games with Ray. It'll relax you."

"Okay," I say, nodding. "Maybe I'll give him a sponge bath, too. Anything else I can do for your little friend?"

JC looks at me as he gets into his car. "Fuck off, Watson."

I wave to him hap-hap-happily. "And fuck you very much, JC."

I slam the door so I don't have to look at his smug, laid back bumper as it rolls easily around the corner. Is there some kind of reverse Stockholm Syndrome that makes kidnappers start to sympathize with their victims? If so, JC has—

"How about that sponge bath, sweetheart?" calls Ray from downstairs. "I'm ready when you are."

This is unbearable.

twelve

"What the fuck do you think you're doing?" I say. I try to grab the laptop back from Ray, but the bastard is holding on tight.

"Just let me do an e-mail," says Ray. He is fighting me off with his elbow and trying to type one-handed at the same time. "The son of a bitch is trying to steal my job and I won't have it."

I push the laptop closed on his fingers and grab it firmly with both hands. "Write it down. You don't get to e-mail, remember?" He still is not letting go and we look at each other for a moment. "Let go, Ray."

"He's making a play," he says. He stops tugging. "I need to be there."

"Let go. Write down what you want to say and I will e-mail everyone you want to carbon copy, blind copy and double forward with additional comments. Just let go."

Ray is sitting there with his two hands on the laptop like it's his job that he's holding onto. He is looking into my eyes, but I see that he's running it through in his mind and not really seeing me. Finally he lets go. "Give me some paper," he says.

I take the laptop and get up from the couch. "Thank-you. I will get you some paper and we will deal with this. So tell me what we're facing here." I put the laptop on the other couch across from Ray and, since he's just sitting there looking like a dude who just got told by his doctor that he has three weeks to live, I walk over and get the pad of paper that's on the table by his elbow and put it in his lap. He doesn't move, so I get him the pen, too. "Ray, speak to me, buddy. What is it? Who cares what some assistant editor thinks?"

"Gerald Spooner is not just some assistant editor. He's my right hand, go-to guy. I brought him along from the beginning. I hired him out of university… all he had was a Masters in Fine Art. He had no useful skills, no work experience, but I could see that he loved comic strips. He'd still be working at Starbucks if it wasn't for me."

"Good. Let it out."

"He's sending me a message. He's sowing the seeds of doubt in their minds. Calling my judgment into question. And I didn't even greenlight the damn thing." He grabs the pen and pad and throws them at the bookcase, getting caught up in his leg chains. He pulls them over the end of the couch to give himself more slack. "Fuck me. I passed on it."

"That's it. Pretend I'm not here."

"Oh, sorry. But you know what I mean."

"Sure."

The e-mail arrived sometime after JC stormed off and I had cleaned up the lunch stuff and sat down to pick up Ray's voice mails. Basically, no one was calling him anymore. We turned the ringer off and just replied by e-mail to anyone that called and left a voice mail. So they got the idea and started e-mailing instead. At first he was getting all voice messages and no e-mails and now it was the opposite, which was a lot easier for us. Along with our own launch, we had to deal with the other minutiae of Ray's office life: 50/50 draws, walks for breast cancer, pornographic pictures from some guy in Accounting, updates from other cartoonists including the guy we relegated to the back burner, some contract stuff with the lawyers, and on and on. Mostly he just told us what to say on the important stuff and we ignored the rest.

When it first arrived, I didn't think much of it because Ray was always getting e-mails from Gerald. Despite his many questions, Gerald had been executing most of what we were preparing for the launch. We uploaded all the strip files for him to have the graphics department prepare them for printing, we got him to issue all the checks to pay for the grand plans we had for the launch and generally we relied on him for everything Ray would normally do if he was back at the office. Even his subject line was bland and unremarkable: "Pretzel Logic strip." If you can't create a little drama in the header, what's the point of blasting your boss in front of the whole company? The guy has no flare whatsoever.

Comic strip syndicates—Royal Features especially —have a lot of support staff to work with all their existing artists and features and get them out on time and in color every single week. They also have the editorial staff to select the best new strips out of the 5000 or so they receive in any given year and a sales staff to sell it to newspaper editors. Most syndicates only launch two or three new strips a year. They will often offer a development deal to bring an artist along to the point where they are ready for launch. If they think a strip is good enough for a development deal, it usually means it will be launched for syndication. So three out of every four development deals go on to get launched for syndication, but then only one of those three strips actually goes on to survive past the first year. It is a killer business.

Most of the problem is all the deadwood on the comics pages—old dinosaur strips where the syndicates hold the rights and they are on their second or third generation of artists, just recycling the same old gags and situations. Because newspaper editors are unwilling to upset readers by taking these old stiffs out of the rotation, they fill up space that could be offered to new artists with fresh looks and original ideas. Even the great Bill Watterson didn't make it through the development period with *Calvin and Hobbes.* His first syndicate didn't think he had what it would take and they allowed his contract to expire without picking it up for a launch. Of course, he was able to send the finished product to other syndicates and eventually make it onto the newspaper pages, but this is the tough environment that exists out there.

I pity the poor bastards who do survive, but end up in the shadow land between real success and the kind of numbers that would cause the syndicate to start to lose money and cancel your contract. The sort of cartoonists who are in 75 to 100 papers and make middling service sector type money, but still have to work the long hours in order to keep up with the never ending deadlines. They get no time off and don't even get to sell book collections or get any real recognition for their work. Ask me a year ago and I'd've traded places with those idiots in a second. I would go as long as the syndicate would keep me out there... ten newspapers, twenty. Just to be in the funny pages. That's what scares me about this launch and that's the reason I am working so hard to make sure it is a huge success. Otherwise I am dooming myself to a life of servitude: doing what I love, but at a ridiculous slave wage. We signed a fifteen-year contract, so the pain will be long lasting.

One of the reasons we went with Royal instead of the other offer we received was because they have a traveling sales force. Six people who actually go out with your strip package in hand and sit down with comics page editors to discuss its merits. Most syndicates rely on mailing out packages and following up with telemarketers. So when we are preparing all of our materials for launch, we are preparing the final sales package that would be given to that sales team at the conference (their meeting is in four days, holy shit), after which they would be loosed on the newspaper world, taking the editors by storm.

All these people we needed to rely on to get our strip out there into the world just got an e-mail from this Gerald Spooner snake, the Brutus of our story so far, saying that he—

My cell phone rings. Jesus, what now?

"Hello?"

"Hello, Watson. It's Massimo De Luca."

"Massimo, my man. How are you?"

"Good, good. I'm—"

"Did you—"

"Go ahead."

"What?" I love cell phones.

"Sorry. You first."

"Did you get the pink slips I left for you?"

"Yes, thanks a lot. I'm driving my new baby right now."

"I'm totally jealous. How does it feel?"

"Fantastic. The engine just purrs, Watson. And the interior is like a home theater."

"Stop it, you're killing me." Get to the point, Massimo.

He laughs an evil laugh. "So, the reason I'm calling

is because I haven't heard back from you about my business insurance. It expires on Saturday and you told me my old company won't cover me anymore because of my municipal work. Which I still don't understand. What's the difference? It's still pipes and plumbing, right?"

Shit, I know exactly where that file is in the stacks of paper on my desk. I forgot all about it. That's no problem. I'll call the underwriter and ask for a one-week extension to give me some time to place it with another market. "Yes, it is. But you've got a big exposure to get drawn in on Pollution Liability because of those back-flow preventers you install in plants where they might leak hazardous materials into the municipal water supply. It's not a problem to get it covered, but the company you were with just does insurance for plumbing in homes and offices and such."

"If you say so. That's why I come to the insurance expert."

"You've got that right. I'll get an extension and give you a call next week with the new price, which will be higher, I'm just warning you."

"What? You're killing me, here. The price on the Lexus is already way up."

"Good thing you're making the big bucks, right?"

"I've got expenses, man. And do you know how much tax I pay? If I moved my business to Michigan, I'd pay less than half in corporate tax. I could set up an office in Port Huron and still do work in London."

Yeah, cry me a river, rich boy. "That's Canada for you. We've got to pay for all this public health care and whatnot."

"Don't get me started on public health care."

"I won't. I won't. Listen, I'll let you go, but I'll get

back to you as soon as I know something about your policy."

"Okay, thanks, guy."

"Talk to you soon."

"Bye."

Maybe I can make a few calls tomorrow and just bind on the spot without an extension. I'll have to call Beth and get her to send a few e-mails for me.

From: "Gerald Spooner" <gerald.spooner@royalfeatures.com >

To: "Ray Bennett" <ray.bennett@royalfeatures.com>

Cc: "Cornelia S. Muller" <cornelia.muller@royalfeatures.com>; "Kate Orr" <kate.orr@royalfeatures.com>; "Alicia Martinez" <alicia.martinez@royalfeatures.com>; "Nick Reyes" <nick.reyes@royalfeatures.com>; "John Beltran" <jbeltran@durstmedia.com>

Sent: Thursday, January 29th, 2009 1:37 PM

Subject: Pretzel Logic strip

Ray, I hope you are feeling better. I tried to call you to discuss this strip, but I can't get you, so it looks like I will have to put my thoughts in writing. I couldn't understand it when you made the switch to this other strip a week ago and decided to put "Daily Bread" on the shelf. But I told myself I would give it time to see how it went. Now that I have worked on it for a week, I find I understand it even less. I don't even remember talking to you about this strip, let alone feeling that it was an up and comer and was ready for launch. Where did it come from? Why hasn't it been vetted by the Editorial Group as we normally would?

I'm not sure that this strip will fly given the situation right now. The economy will be a barrier, with several of our most supportive newspapers having gone out of business and ad revenues down significantly. We would have had a hard push with "Daily Bread" and religion and stocks are red hot right now.

It will be hard to get newspaper editors' attention to begin with, but to be going out there with a reworded yoga strip after how quickly the bottom has fallen out of the yoga market… I just can't see it. Pilates will be dead in a month. It will be like Tae Bo all over again.

For these reasons, I respectfully withdraw my support for "Pretzel Logic." I think we should all meet to see where we're at. Even if you could come in and hear people's opinions, it might be beneficial. If you still can't talk, you could write something down or type on a computer. Do you think you're feeling up to coming into the office? We all want to work through this with you. Let us know where you stand.

Sincerely,

Gerald S.

"Dear Gerald," says Ray. He is staring at the dark TV screen. "You are an ungrateful little weasel. I am Ray Bennett. If I say this will fly, it will fly."

"Who is John Beltran?" I say, looking up from the laptop.

"That's our contact at corporate. It means that Gerald is trying to fuck me."

"Yikes. Why don't we fuck him instead, then?"

"Yes. That's what we'll do."

I walk over to the bookcase and pick up the pen and paper off the floor. "You write. I'll make us some coffee. Let's word this just perfectly so they have no doubt about what we're doing and lots of doubts about Gerald."

He takes the pad and pen from me and sets them in his lap. "Perfect."

I take the steps two at a time. I'm actually relieved that this is out. I knew there would be some resistance and I'm surprised it took this long for someone to come right

144

out and oppose the abrupt change. Now all we have to do is squelch this objection and we're home free. I set up the coffee maker and get out some cinnamon buns from the box. I love having an emergency to work through. It gives me a sense of purpose and also something I can handle in JC's absence to show him how much he needs me. And who doesn't love coffee and a sense of purpose when they're feeling powerless and oddly conflicted about everything? I love the smell of cinnamon in the afternoon —it smells like victory.

Missing Person – Initial Report

CONFIDENTIAL

Case Name/Number *NY17/23012009/8349* **Agency** *NYPD, 17th Precinct*	
Date *01-29-2009* **Time** *16:30*	**Information taken by** *PO Neil Kakaadjan*
Caller's Name *Gerald Spooner*	**Call-back number** *212-234-2344*
Address *592 Warwick St, Brooklyn, NY*	
Home Phone *718-342-7320*	**Business Phone** *212-234-2344*
Cell Phone, Other Numbers *917-253-4637*	
Relationship to missing person *Employee*	
Reason for reporting this person missing *Strange behavior at work, started using e-mail all of a sudden, not answering phone, says he is home sick with laryngitis, no answer at door, GPS on work cell phone says it is located in London, Canada, he has suddenly started championing a comic strip by two artists from this same city, Mr. Spooner fears he has been kidnapped.*	

Missing Person

Full Name *Ray Bennett*	**Nickname(s)** *None*
Subject's primary language *English*	
Home address *312 E 75th Street, NY, NY*	
Home Phone *646-852-4627*	**Business Phone** *212-969-3975*
Cell Phone, Other Numbers *917-951-2386*	

Description

Age	Race	Gender	M	Hgt	5'9"	Wgt	DOB
52	Wht					205	10/27/56

General Description and Clothing Worn When Last Seen

Navy pants, blue pinstriped shirt, deck shoes, green coat. Balding, medium height, thick around the

middle, sometimes wears white socks with dark shoes.

Details of Loss

Location missing from   *Durst Tower Office Building, 298 W 57th St, NY, NY, 10019, 14th Floor*

Point Last Seen (PLS)   *In his office*

Day/Date Last Seen   *Friday, January 23rd, 2009*   **Time Last Seen**   *17:30*

Last seen by whom   *Receptionist, Vera Frankovich*

Vehicle description, if driving   *N/A*

Destination(s), stated intentions   *None – assumed to be going home that evening*

Has this person been the object of a search in the past?   *No*

If so, describe date(s), circumstances of loss, how long missing, when found, where found, condition when found and actions taken by subject while missing (if known)

Additional Information and Comments

Buzzed out of building using passcard at 6:30pm, security video shows patient being transported in

wheelchair at that time wearing Mets cap, incident report log from cleaning staff says they found a

janitor's uniform in the trash in missing person's office and logged in lost and found on the 25th.

Call-out Information

Search base/command post location, directions, phone numbers, radio frequencies:

Check for parking tickets and driving citations on the date in question.

Resources notified: *FBI.*

Closing Report

Subject Location:	Date	Time
Located By:		
Incident Summary:		

thirteen

It is after 9:00 on my dashboard clock as I am parking in front of my house. We got everything straightened out back at the New York office. We put Gerald in his place and defended our strip's honor admirably. By the time Monday rolls around, everyone will be ready to hand off the launch kits to the sales staff and get them all pumped up about Pilates. Ray was amazing. He was tenacious and unbending and really knew how to stick the knife in where it hurts. We have corporate convinced this is the best strip we've launched in years and worth every penny of the, ahem, large sums we have committed for trade advertising support and glossy folders.

And we accomplished all this without any help from JC. Not even a phone call. It's probably for the best right now. Let him cool off a bit. I click the button on my key fob and listen for the clunk of the car doors locking. Walk up my front steps picking through all my other keys thinking: office, shed, Mom and Dad's place, bike lock, back door, desk drawer, screen door, don't know, don't remember, front door? I wish someone would make a key fob for a house so I could just click the button and open my front door lock. Maybe someday they will. I guess that's the way the security passes work when they unbolt an electromagnetic lock. Maybe I could get one of those installed on my house.

I open the door and step into the front hall. The house is dark, so I turn on a light to hang up my coat and put away my shoes and wallet and stuff in the closet. It's not even 9:30, but I guess Jess packed it in early. Or maybe she went out or something? I look around as I'm heading towards the kitchen and stop. She's sitting in the living room in the dark.

"Hi, sweetie," I say. "What's going on?"

She just looks at me steadily. Something is wrong. She's been crying. She's kind of dressed up. What could have happened? Did someone die? Or did I forget our anniversary or what? I was supposed to do something. What were we talking about this morning? Date. *Oh shit.*

"Oh, honey, I'm so sorry. I forgot all about our date tonight. We had a huge issue with the strip come up today and we had to do damage control with some loser in the New York office. I took the afternoon off work to clean up the mess and I just lost track of time. Of everything."

"You didn't call," she says. "You didn't text." Surprisingly calm. Maybe too calm.

"I'm a shit. I can't believe it slipped my mind. I'm just so caught up in all this launch stuff."

"Caught up in what's important to you."

"You're important." I'm kind of frozen, but I feel like I should be moving in for a hug.

"Stay where you are."

How does she do that? "Nothing is as important to me as you are. I've just gone... temporarily crazy. I'm under a lot of pressure right now." Again, I won't knock it. Temporary Insanity might make a good plea someday.

"This comic strip is the best thing that ever happened to you. I get it."

"Well, yeah, but... no, I mean, you're the best thing that ever happened to me."

"Uh-huh." She looks away from me, which is its own kind of communication.

"Let me make it up to you. Let's go out right now. Or tomorrow night. We could go to a club and I'll even dance."

"You're going to make it up to me for missing a date that was supposed to make it up to me that you've been absent from our marriage."

"I wouldn't say I've been absent from our marriage. I've just been really busy and stressed out for the last week."

"I have no idea that you're stressed. You never talk to me about it. I never know what's going on because you don't share it with me. You've been absent for a long time."

"Really? Because I thought we were just talking about this week. That's okay. Go ahead, read the charges. How long has this alienation of affection been going on, Mrs. Sinclair?"

"A joke. What a nice change. Will this be in your strip?"

"What's a joke is that I can't get any support from you on something that is this important to me. Just a little slack would be all I need."

"And now you're turning it around on me and I'm the bad guy. Right on schedule. I'm tired of having the same old fights, Watson. We need some new material."

Even that is an old dig. I sit down on the chair opposite her and just look at her. I'm so tired. Fighting is such a waste of energy.

"Don't sit down—you're not staying."

"What?" What's this?

"We need some time apart. I can't take this right

now."

"Fine, I'll sleep on the couch."

"No, I want you out of here. I don't want to look at you."

"Where am I supposed to go?"

"Go where you always go: your parents' house. You're practically living there anyway; just make it official."

I've had to ride the couch plenty of times since we've been married, but never have I been asked to leave the domicile. This is new. "Really? You want me to leave?"

"We need some time apart, Watson."

"What's that supposed to accomplish?"

"Maybe we'll decide we miss each other and we're better off together."

"Or?"

"Or maybe it feels better to be apart and we start talking about making it permanent."

Wow. How did we get here? "Feels better for who? Sounds like you're the one making all these decisions."

"We both get a say in our future together. That's just the way it works."

"Well, why should I be the one to leave?"

"Oh, don't be a baby. You know why."

"I'll give you the key to my parents' place... you go stay there." Oops, I mean, shit. No she can't.

"Don't mess with me, Watson. I've had a long time to think about this while I was waiting around for three hours for you to show up." There goes the calm. I was tired of it anyway.

"And all you came up with was, 'Kick Watson out?' I figured you'd have a lawyer already here with you."

"You bastard! Don't you dare joke about that!"

"Oh, relax. You'll live longer."

"I can't believe you're acting this way."

"Oh, I'm not acting. I am this way."

She is shaking with rage, but I somehow don't care. Maybe I'm enjoying it. She says, "Is our marriage over?"

"You seem to think it is."

"Get out!" She stands up and points at the door, looking a bit like Godzilla emerging from the water.

"Okay," I say, standing up sarcastically. "You're so scary I have to run right out of here!"

"When you act like an asshole, it just makes this easier."

"I've tried nice. It gets me nowhere."

She's standing there glaring at me and those flames shooting out of her eyes are going to singe her perfect eyebrows, which were expensive. I'm squaring off with her toe to toe, ready with some other choice insults. This feels good, like I've been angry for days, weeks, months without being able to let it out. Well, it's coming out now and I like it. And then that hard look of rage on her face fractures, weakened by a frisson near her lip and then she's crying and running out of the room.

"Just go," she says on the way.

I watch her go up the stairs and then into the bedroom, not even slamming the door. That bitch. She's not playing fair. I look around the room for something that I can break. Why don't we have more china knick-knacks? So critical at a time like this. What am I supposed to do now, go up there and comfort her? Or stomp out in anger? I can feel myself weakening because of the tears and I need to feed the fire or I'm going to lose it altogether. And just by thinking that, it's gone in a rush of breath and a plume of smoke. I swallow my adrenaline into a hard lump in my throat. This is not healthy. I walk over to the stairs and put my foot on the first step.

"You'll only make it worse."

That is some supernatural shit. When does a marriage turn into competitive mind reading? Well, fuck me. That was well played. This is why I so seldom win any of our fights: she's just so good at it. I'm out of options. And yet tired. I'll sleep over at my parents' place for one night and then bring flowers and chocolates tomorrow for the dance of contrition. I can't believe I forgot about our date. I must be losing my mind. It was just this morning that the idea got me out of a jam and by mid-afternoon it had escaped me completely. It's all Gerald Spooner's fault. He really is a fucking weasel.

I turn out the light in the front hall, close the door behind me and lock it. I use my key fob to open my car door and it welcomes me with little lights on everywhere. At least my car understands my needs. The engine sits up and looks at me. *Back again, sir? Are we going for another ride? I thought we were put in for the night. Does her Royal Highness want a particular flavor of ice cream for Letterman?* I turn the key and the engine busies itself with its pistons and spark plugs and whatever.

I can't remember my parents ever fighting when I was a kid. I mean, they must have, but they were very quiet about it. I never saw my dad sleeping on the couch or moving out of the house for a trial separation. How did they do it? And how were they always able to afford groceries and vacations and still put money away for a rainy day? I never saw them paying off one credit card bill with another credit card. It's possible they did, but I wouldn't bet on it.

There has been some kind of breakdown in the way

relationship information is passed from one generation to the next. Fifty percent of marriages end in divorce now. People have no clue how to compromise and give and take and listen and relate anymore. Marriage is in trouble and that's why I think our comic strip will be such an important vehicle to teach the lessons I've learned to readers. Hard lessons with an edge of humor. Because if I'm separated before my comic strip about marriage even hits newspapers, that will be bad, but probably humorous to someone.

All the songs on the radio are upbeat pop numbers about girls and guys getting together. Not one about heartbreak and despair. I can't stand this, but my only other option is the country and western station or silence, so I stick with it. I hum absently all the way to my parents' house. I open the front door and turn on a light. Hang my coat on the doorknob and look in the mirror. That is the face of a failed husband. I screwed up tonight—not Jessica. Although she went eight kinds of psycho about it, including the weird tears of rage. What kind of hormones does it take to pull that off?

"Did you forget something?" says Ray from downstairs.

Yes. I suck in breath through my lips and then see a black sesame seed between my front teeth and remember that I don't have my toothbrush.

"Hello? Who's there?"

What's my name? Where is my focus? I wouldn't have a strip about marriage if I weren't married to my soul mate, best friend, coolest chick, hot as the 1st of July with all the fireworks, snuggle monkey at the end of the day, tickle marauder after the alarm goes off...

"Watson? Is that you?"

My little wifey. I have really screwed this up. A tear, followed by another, and then one from the other eye, shoots straight down my cheek. It's funny; I have never been able to picture a strip where James was crying.

fourteen

This is the kind of thing that Jess is saying: *You've been sleeping with her. How can I trust you?*

Who? I say, not having a clue, but feeling an aching sense of guilt for hurting her, so it must be true, I realize. *Who told you?*

Your mother told me all about it.

How would she know?

She knows. And now I know and we're finished.

I've never been unfaithful, not even once, I say, recovering. I reach out for her but I get caught in the blankets instead.

The upstairs guest room. My parents' house. 10:15am. It took me forever to get to sleep last night and I guess I didn't bother to set an alarm. My head throbs with the tension of opposites: the greatest artistic success of my life in Monday's launch of our strip to the sales team and the dismal, hopeless feeling of personal failure in my marriage. It's hard to focus on the two simultaneously and the tension is splitting my brain down the middle.

How am I going to fix this? Ouch. Thinking hurts. Step One: apologize. Step Two: flowers and grovelling. Step Three? This didn't happen in one week. It was a long time coming. Figure it out. Think it through… it's not the fight. The engine of our marriage has always run on internal combustion, but that isn't what's wrong here. It's the lack of maintenance — that's the problem. Routine, day-to-day stuff. Twenty-eight grams of prevention is worth 454 grams of cure. One rose a week rather than a dozen when I screw up. I can do that. It will be better when the launch is over.

I reach over to the nightstand for my cell phone and text her a message. *So sorry. Screwd up. No sleep. Miss U. Beautiful.* The literature of future worlds will be authors texting their readers on cell phones: *2 B or not 2 B? That is the ?* Will we call that literacy? I think we will. As I sit waiting for Jess to text me back, I decide to text JC as well. *Dude. How goes? Major fix-up yest. Call me.* Should probably apologize to him, too, but I'm not buying him flowers. He'll get over it. He's pretty easy-going. Lucky 4 me.

Better make some coffee. I put on my pants from yesterday over my underwear from yesterday and trudge down the hall and down the stairs. Ray is awake and reading a book.

"Morning," he says.

"Morning. Coffee?"

"Yeah."

"Cool." Tired of trudging, I decide to try shuffling instead, and I like the sound it makes better. I mount the long staircase slowly, making hand over hand contact with the railing, and I finally reach the top. I have to take a moment in the front hall because the changes in altitude are allowing the pain to slice into virgin territory in my brain matter. The bright light coming through the windows up here isn't helping. And now my phone. Perfect. It won't be Jess, of course.

"Hello?"

"Watson? Where the hell are you?" The boss man.

"At home. I slept in."

160

"Jesus Christ, this is just what I've been talking about. First you're gone all afternoon yesterday and—"

"I know. I'm sick. I was hoping I could sleep it off, but I'm going to spend the day in bed and be good as new on Monday."

"Do you know I haven't taken a sick day in over 32 years? You don't build a business by being sick all the time."

"I will tell that to the flu bug what bit me."

"Flu bug. Huh. Is that what you're calling it? Hungover is what we used to say and we'd work it off. Have you tried a raw egg and Tabasco in tomato juice?"

"I'm not hungover, but thanks for your concern."

"All right, but I'd better see your car in the parking lot when I pull in at 7:30 Monday morning."

"There is no chance of that, but I'll be there by 9:00."

"You'd better be."

I hang up and check for new texts from Jess or JC. Nothing. Is it too much to ask that people keep their phones on at work and get back to you right away? I get on with making the coffee and while it's going through I make some toast. I love the smell of toast and coffee. It makes my head feel better. Who needs expensive aromatherapy when you've got this stuff? Once it's all ready, I look at the two cups and two plates and realize I will have to use a tray or make two trips. I find it very unmanly to enter a room with a tray, but I'm too tired to go up and down the stairs twice, so I opt for the Julia Child route.

Ray puts down his book when he sees me coming with the tray. He seems happy to see a breakfast that isn't FRICKIN' GRANOLA BARS, about which he complains all the time. Bloody whiner; he's lucky it's not just bread and water, as served in prisons everywhere.

And he hasn't eaten much of the fruit, so it's his own fault.

"Coffee's not bad," he says.

"It's better once you get used to having it black. You really taste the coffee."

"Yeah, yeah. I'll still switch to cream and sugar again when I'm back at the office." We exchange glances and non-verbal information simultaneously and then both look away. We haven't talked about his return for a few days and I'm sure it's crossed his mind a lot as we get closer to the launch date.

"So what are you going to do?" he says. "I mean, are you kicked out for good or are you going to kiss and make up or what?"

I sit back, cradling my coffee to my chest. "If I knew, I'd tell you, brother."

"Wow. How ironic."

"Yes, I'm aware of the irony. You don't have to go over it again."

"Sorry." He takes a sip of coffee and his eyes flick to the clock on the digital cable box. "So you're not going to work?"

"Nah. I don't feel much like working and I figure I might as well hang out here in case your little buddy tries to pull another fast one."

"This late in the game? After we already shut him down? I can't see it, but who knows."

"I'm ready either way. Worst case scenario, I sit here and have some toast with peanut butter and then grab a nap."

* * *

162

After trying to call her four or five times, Jess finally texts me around 1:30. All she says is, *I need space.* So I decide to swing by the house to grab a few things and lay the groundwork for my return to her good graces. I buzz by the Metro on the way and pick up a colorful bunch of flowers. I write "Sorry" on the card and leave them in a vase on our kitchen table.

I sit and look around our kitchen for a minute, not knowing what to do next. I've been carrying Ray's cell phone with me so I can check the messages periodically, so I do that now just to have something to do. No voice mail. No texts.

I pack some clothes in a duffel bag in case this lasts the weekend or longer. I remember to pack my toiletries kit as well as my electric razor. I switch coats to my fleece-lined Gore-Tex because the temperature has warmed up and they are calling for rain. I make the bed. I lie down on top of the comforter and stare at the ceiling for a while. I am planning a romantic weekend getaway to a spa and country inn which is a little over an hour north of London. Forget chocolates; massages are the way to go. Massages and toe varnish.

If I think back, though, things have been mostly good between us. Yes, I have neglected her this past week. Yes, I forgot an important date, but did it really warrant all this divorce talk? I feel like we have a good marriage, overall. We have fun together. We like a lot of the same things, and we laugh a lot. We're both faithful, despite what my subconscious thinks. When she gets upset with me, I sometimes have no idea what she's angry about and she calls me clueless and gets over it.

Isn't it the same in all heterosexual relationships?

The root is hetero, meaning "different," as in, "not the same." *Men are from Mars and women are from Venus*, as the self-helpful tomes would have us believe. Which is a great idea, now that I think on it. I will get a copy of that book to show her I'm really trying. I like it. Call it a crash course in Venutian for a well-intentioned but confused Martian. I still think she could have cut me a little slack in view of how important this project is to me. I have a point, here. There is another side to the story. But people who get too wrapped up in who's right end up telling it to a judge.

I never see JC going through this kind of stuff. Sylvie is cool with whatever he does. To the point of not caring. But she is a really laid back person, anyway, so it makes sense. Most of the time when we go out with them she will just sit there and listen to conversations we'll be having and not have much to say, but once in a blue moon she'll get in a groove on some subject and you could just let her go and she would talk for hours. JC would look really intently at her and always be stroking her arm or playing with her hair, but actually listening, too. You could tell he was really into her. With her I wasn't so sure.

But JC can do whatever he wants, whenever. He can be out at the bar with me one night and go to the movies the next and he never gets any flak about it like I would if I went out without Jess a couple of nights in one week. She'd be saying how come you don't take me to the bar or how come we don't go to the movies? Just you and me. Sylvie never seemed to care either way. Part of it was that she had about a thousand hours of reading a week for her program, which I don't really completely get. But I also feel like part of it is her. That she is just cold and doesn't care enough about JC.

If this is true, JC doesn't seem to notice. They get

along well and whatever they have together works for them, but I like that Jess is a little more passionate about me and wants me around a lot. It's kind of nice most of the time. If I was married to Sylvie, I'd almost feel like, what the fuck is the point? She's with me, she's not with me— she doesn't give two shits either way. I'm not saying she isn't hot, because she works that French sexy angle like there's no tomorrow and the day after that is looking iffy, too, so I get the attraction piece. But where does that get you when the sex is over?

Who knows what goes on inside other people's marriages? Things always look different from the outside looking in. I'm sure people look at Jess and me and think all we do is bicker with each other. I think that sometimes. But that's just us. At least it's out on the table and not festering. Although some stuff clearly has been festering or she wouldn't be this worked up. But she'll get over it. She always does. This is one comfortable bed. How could anyone wake up angry after sleeping on this?

News from home

Elaine Bissell <elainebissell@sympatico.ca>
Reply-To: Elaine Bissell <elainebissell@sympatico.ca>
To: Marnie Sinclair <marnie.sinclair@gmail.com>

Hi, Marnie. It's Elaine here. Hope your weather is nice and
you and George are having a good time in Florida. It is wet
and cold here, as always. They say it will warm up enough
for freezing rain on the weekend. I wish I could be where you
are, but somebody had to have us all tied up in stocks last
year right before the crash if you can believe it.

I just wanted to let you know that your son Watson has been
spending a lot of time at your house lately. I know for a fact
that he slept there twice last weekend and again last night,
as I happened to get up in the middle of the night and looked
out the window and saw his car. And it was still there early
this morning and most of the day today.

I just worry that he is having trouble at home and has now
moved out. I thought you'd want to know, as I know you've
had your suspicions in the past about how that Jessica treats
him. I know he isn't likely to call you for help himself, so you
mightn't know otherwise.

Please excuse the intrusion if you feel it is none of your
business. It was kindly intended. See you in the spring!

Elaine Bissell
#14

fifteen

Jess finds the flowers and is instantly enchanted. *Did you get these at Metro?*

Metro? What, oh... you mean the A&P?

Yeah, they changed it a while back.

Why?

It doesn't matter, I just wanted you to know that their flowers are the best you can get from a non-florist retailer.

I know, I say. *I've always felt that way. And you deserve the best that a non-florist retailer has to offer.*

Baby, how can I stay mad at you?

You can't.

But when I wake up, still in the guest room at my parent's house, I realize she can and she will. Who knows when this exile will end? Oh, well. It's Saturday, so maybe she'll have time to talk things out with her sister or a girlfriend or something and they'll tell her that we're all the same, you might as well stick with this one, because at least he doesn't cheat or abuse you or run up gambling debts. This is my niche: the "Not as Bad as it Could Be" Zone. I'm the top dog in this particular arena.

I get up, make coffee, eat some toast and a banana and watch the sports news with Ray. It feels strange to just be sitting around doing not much. There's probably something we could be working on for Monday, but it feels really good to be relaxing. I'm wicked tired after all the craziness of the last eight days. Maybe I'll take a nap.

Ray is trying to convince me that he's a big Knicks fan, but he probably followed them for about five minutes during a title run back in Patrick Ewing's day. The only current player he seems to know is David Lee.

We're having our second coffees and talking about playing some Crazy Taxi or something when I hear the front door open and JC call down. I head up the stairs and say hey as he's taking off his coat.

"Hey," I say.

"Hey," he says. He opens the closet to hang up his coat, his back to me. When he turns around he looks at me standing there like he knows what's coming.

"So, are we cool?" I say.

He shrugs. "Sure."

"Good," I say. "Coffee?"

"Sure." He follows me down the hall to the kitchen. "What's with the bedhead?"

"Slept here." Not a story I'm fond of telling, really. It hurts to admit this to myself, let alone other people.

"Why? What were you guys working on?"

"Nothing." I pull a mug out of the cupboard for him and pour the last of the coffee. How to explain this? "Okay, so the thing is, Jessica kind of... asked me to leave. So I came here."

He looks at me while absorbing this. "When did this happen?" He takes a sip of coffee and leans up against the counter.

"Thursday, but it goes back further. Basically this whole week she's been feeling neglected, for obvious reasons. We've had some fights about it and Thursday morning I tried to make it up to her by promising to take her out to dinner and a movie. Pretty lame that it's the best I've got. I've gotta up my game when this is all over, you know?"

"You?" He shrugs one of those all-encompassing French Canadian shrugs that says, *No way, you're okay, what's to worry about, where do women get these ideas, anyway, and why are we responsible for their delusions, dinner and a movie out is one of the greatest little pleasures life has to offer and to share that with someone you love is amazing and real, not some fantasy from a romance book that is as elusive as it is exasperating, you're a good husband who tries hard, what the heck, sacré bleu, tabernac, qu'est que c'est?*

"Yeah, I know. But I feel like she deserves better, so I'm going to try to be better when I get a second chance. If I get another chance."

"Seriously? She's that mad?"

"Oh, she's pretty steamed. Okay, so dinner and a movie Thursday. After I blew up at you that afternoon, which we've already covered, I hung out here for a while and we got an e-mail from Gerald saying he withdraws his support from the strip and thinks we should can it."

"No way," he says. "That weasel. So that was the fix-up you texted me about?"

"Yeah. And he cc'd everybody at Royal and their contact at corporate just for good measure. A real 'fuck-you.' So we spent the rest of the day sending e-mails giving Gerald the smack-down and providing support for the strip. Ray was brilliant, by the way. He took it really personally that Gerald would question his judgment, so he really helped me stick it to him."

"And you lost track of time and forgot all about the date."

"Bingo. So I get home after 9:00 and we have a big blow up and she says get out. So I came here and hardly slept at all. I called in sick yesterday and tried to call her fifty times. All I got back was a text saying 'I need space.'"

JC takes a sip of coffee, looking at the pictures on my Mom's fridge, then nodding. "At least it wasn't 'It's over.'"

"True. But she's pretty worked up about it. Let's head back downstairs... I still have half a coffee down there. I really don't know what's making her so upset. I got the eerie calm, the shouting rage and then the tears all in about two minutes. I could swear we've gone weeks when she's working on a big campaign that I've seen less of her than she's seen of me this week. Where's the support, right? Where's the love when it's my turn?"

"Good point," says JC.

Ray is looking up at us as we get down there. He has Sportsdesk on mute on the big screen and the report has moved on to curling, which I'm sure he never sees on ESPN. "Morning, Frenchie," he says to JC. "Did you hear our boy's sad story?"

I sit back down on my couch against the wall and JC takes the spot on Ray's couch which is in between the two of us. He puts his coffee down on the coaster on the end table, which would make my Mom very happy if she didn't notice the hole in the drywall.

"Yeah, Brooklyn," says JC. "I heard. You helping him keep his spirits up?"

"Oh, yeah. We've been talking it out. Right, Watson?"

"Uh-huh. You know what JC didn't say when I told him? He didn't say how ironic it is that my marriage is breaking up."

"Oooh," says JC, wincing. "I never thought of that. It is kind of ironic."

"All right," I say. "Spare me the irony. Anyway, my

marriage is not breaking up."

"You're right," says Ray. "This is pretty tame stuff. I slept on the couch at work for a while when my marriage was breaking up, but it got much worse."

"That sucks," says JC.

"Marriage is hard," says Ray. "I don't know how people do it."

"Well, that's what our strip was about," says JC. "Before we added all the yoga and now pilates nonsense. It was supposed to be about what it's like inside a marriage."

"No question," says Ray. "And you do it well."

"Hey," I say. "We should do a bunch of strips about marital issues. Show them arguing, but what's funny is the futility of it, the lack of substance of their disagreements. And James sleeping on the couch and asking his father for advice and stuff. Give the humor an edge of reality."

"I think you could pull that off," says JC. He reaches out a fist and I bump it.

"That could work," says Ray. "If it was my issue, he'd be caught staring at one of the hotties in his pilates class and the wife would notice."

"No wonder you had strife," says JC. "You've gotta be subtle about that stuff."

"If I asked my Dad for advice about marriage," I say. "First he would need to know how I could have screwed things up like this. It would be totally alien to him."

"But the father in the strip would be all too familiar with marital strife," says JC.

"That's one area that needs work," says Ray. "The parents seem like cardboard cutout wealthy parents."

"Agree," I say. "They're not modeled on my parents. My parents' marriage seems hard to imagine as two

172

individuals. It's like an entity preordained and formed out of bedrock. A couple in the singular sense. A marital unit, indivisible."

"Mine broke up when I was seven," says JC. "So I know a little bit about divisibility and marital strife."

"Mine were pretty good together," says Ray. "Not a lot of fighting. I seemed to figure that out on my own. Didn't need someone to model it for me."

"Will you look at us," says JC. "Talking about relationships like a bunch of women. Isn't there some wrestling on TV or anything?"

"Sure," I say. "There's gotta be."

"Well, that means we need nachos," says Ray. He starts flicking through the channel guide. "Can't have wrestling without nachos."

I stand up and grab my empty coffee cup and move towards the stairs. "Coming up."

* * *

"I can't believe it's your big week and she won't even talk to you. That's bullshit, man."

"You know?"

"Damn straight."

"More beer?"

"More beer!"

"Number nine and number ten."

"I love this Canadian beer, man. It makes my gums feel loose and my tongue is all sparkly."

"Alcohol brings out your inner Elmo, man. Too funny."

"I would green light an Elmo strip in a second. Sesame Street is an evergreen property. I also love that your beer is just called 'Canadian.' You guys keep it simple, doncha?"

"There's other kinds, too."

"Sure, sure. Plus you smoke tons of pot, right?"

"That's B.C.."

"Oh. Too bad."

"You wanna get your toke on?"

"Abso-frickin-lute-amagootin-ly! Do you know I've never had the munchies?"

"Never?"

"Never. So do you have any?"

"Nope."

"Shit… that's okay. I feel good right now. Real relaxed."

"What?"

"I'm relaxed."

"That's good. I can get you some pretzels if you're hungry."

"No way. I'm good. Do you know that as of this morning I've been here a whole week?"

"Yeah."

"That is amazing. I haven't had a full week off in years."

"No?"

"No. Just long weekends and a few days at Christmas."

"That's sick. How do you survive?"

"I always said that I love my job so much it was like a vacation, but that's bullshit. You know? Is that thunder?"

"Yeah, it is really coming down out there."

"Raining? But it's winter. Where's the snow?"

"It sometimes rains, too. Just to vary the misery."

"But this is Canada."

"Yeah, I know. The fucking igloos must be melting out there, but don't worry. The dog sleds will get through with the supplies."

"Including the beer?"

"Especially the beer. You ready?"

"More beer!"

"Yes, more beer! Jesus, it's the deluge out there. I better check my dad's sump pump. He's had problems with it before. Be right back."

"Okay, but bring more beer. Number ten and number eleven. No, eleven and twelve. Eleventeen and twelveteen."

"So why no time off?"

"What?"

"Why no time off? What you were sayin' before."

"Oh, just because I have no life, man. I work too much so my girlfriends break up with me. Then I have no girlfriend, anyway, so I work more. Then I don't meet any new girlfriends. I'm not good at dating."

"Think you'll ever get married again?"

"Yeah, I think some day I will."

"Yeah?"

"Sure. I read your strip, or even watch some movie, and I think, that's what I'd like to have. Some fun partner to share things with. But women my age can smell a workaholic a mile away. They have too much goddamn dating experience. You can't bullshit them at all."

"You need to find a female workaholic."

"I've tried that. You would think it would work, but not so far. Uptight bitches."

"Who? All of them?"

"No, never mind. Definitely not marriage material."

"I like marriage, but the grass is always greener, right? I can see how batching it would feel good sometimes. Like right now. Just kicking it with my homey."

"Cheers, bro."

"Cheers."

"To a successful launch."

"Success."

"May all the editors' wives do pilates on the weekend."

"That would help."

"Well, it's Saturday night. What's shaking in London? You want to go clubbing?"

"Nice. Why don't we see what's on the movie channel?"

"JC is probably out clubbing with his hot little French number."

"Sylvie is a PhD student. Not sure if she clubs it too much."

"Oh, c'mon. A student who doesn't like to party?"

"JC doesn't like dancing and it's not like it's her birthday."

"But he hasn't been around much this week like you. Maybe he's throwin' her a bone to make it up to her."

"Ha! Too funny. Should we text him?"

"Yes!"

"OK. 'Dude. You clubbin? Ray wants to know.' Send. Let's see what he says."

"JC's a good shit."

"Yeah, he is."

"How long have you guys been compadres?"

"Forever. All through school and whatnot."

"That's great. I don't have any friends left from school. We all moved away."

"Don't you connect on Facebook?"

"Shit, no. I have no time for that crap."

"Where did you grow up, anyway?"

"I grew up in a small town called North Royalton which is near Cleveland."

"Wow, that's just across the lake, then. What did you do in North Royalton for fun?"

"Not much. My dad was a pharmacist and ran the local drugstore. So I would spend a lot of time hanging out there with my friends. He would let us read all the comics for free as long as we didn't mess them up."

"That sounds a lot like me. JC and I always bought our comics at a drugstore not too far from where we went to school."

"I would help my dad put all the comics on the shelves every Thursday. My buddy Charlie Cooper and I would arrange all the comics on the bottom shelf and would always highlight the best comic of the week in a display rack over by the counter. Our comic of the week always sold out."

"Always had the eye, huh?"

"Yeah. And we would try to read all the newspaper strips. My dad carried the Cleveland Plain Dealer, The Columbus Dispatch, the Akron Beacon-Journal, as well as the New York Times and Washington Post. We would have to flip through most of them because this one had Peanuts, but not Blondie. And this one would have Pogo, but not Hagar. There was the Wizard of Id and B.C.... Doonesbury was just starting. Trudeau was the one who introduced me to politics."

"It was comics paradise."

"It was! When I went away to school, I started out in Fine Arts, but switched to Political Science when I realized I didn't have the true talent myself."

"What school did you go to?"

"Columbia."

"Cool. Good school, I hear."

"It was a great school. And a great city. I never moved back to North Royalton after living in Manhattan. How could you?"

"You couldn't."

"I didn't."

"Don't."

"Ha! What do you know, Mr. London-Ontario? Probably lived here all your life. Married your high school sweetheart and live within 6.5 blocks of where you grew up. Statistician's dream!"

"It's all true! What can I say? I guess I love it here."

"Pff. Too comfortable. You need to live in the Big Apple for a while. See what life is really all about."

"Tell me more. I've got to hear this."

"I will. But first…"

"More beer?"

"More beer!"

sixteen

Monday. Launch Day. Going back home day —
whether she likes it or nay. She still hasn't called or
answered any of my texts. It's getting stupid.

Ray and I are sitting around in the den having our
coffees and some celebratory cinnamon buns while we wait
to hear from the New York office, who aren't answering
their e-mails right now. It's 8:15, so they should be there
soon, considering today is the day the sales team from all
over the U.S. will be converging on the Big Apple to get
direction for their next cycle of sales calls. Gerald is
supposed to give the presentation in Ray's absence. It will
be his first presentation, so Ray figures he'll be nervous
and running around doing last minute things. And not e-
mailing us with an update.

"I can't wait much longer or my boss will be
wearing my ass like a hat," I say to Ray. I point to my
watch meaningfully. "Where is this guy?"

"Oh, he's there," says Ray. "He's an early riser like
me. One of the two of us is usually the first in to the
office."

"Is there someone else who might be there who can
let us know what's happening?"

"Don't worry about it. They're professionals... they
do three of these a year."

"Not for me they don't. This is my one shot."

"It'll be fine. Eat your cinnamon bun. They're

delicious."

"Aren't they?"

Ray is sipping coffee and munching on his breakfast, legs crossed, sitting back on the couch like a dowager duchess, comfortable as you please. He has a full beard now, which suits him somehow. He's wearing the NASCAR hoodie and jeans and he looks happy and relaxed. I wish I felt half as relaxed as that. Then my phone rings, which isn't helping. I look at the call display: not Jess, not the office, not J.C., but the number looks familiar.

"Hello?"

"Hello, hi, Watson? This is Massimo."

Massimo? Jesus, it's not even 9:00. "Massimo, how goes it?"

"Terrible. My shop is full of water and sewage and shit."

Shit, oh shit. That's the word. "Oh, my god. The rain."

"Yeah, they had problems with the runoff from melting and the heavy rain in this area. There's wet basements everywhere and my phone is ringing off the hook with emergency work and I can't get at my stuff because it's covered in shit water."

"Yikes. That is shit."

"So, I never heard back from you on Friday about my policy. Where did you place it? Because they aren't going to be happy to find out they have a claim on their hands already."

"No, but that's why we're in business."

"So who should I call?"

"Don't worry about it. I'll call into the office and then call you back."

"Okay. Right away, yes? I want to get someone in here ASAP."

"Oh, yeah." Gulp. I turn to Ray as I hang up. "This comics launch better work out, because I am so fucked at work."

"What's wrong?" says Ray.

"I was supposed to place coverage for a customer on Friday and I didn't and with all the rain on the weekend, his shop is full of sewer water."

"Yuck."

"Yes, yuck."

"So what's going to happen?"

"Well, I don't know. There is no coverage at all for this because I screwed up. Our brokerage has Errors & Omissions Insurance for when we screw up, but the boss won't want to use it because first of all there's a $5000 deductible we'd have to pay. And second, his premiums will go up and it will look like a black mark on the brokerage."

"So who pays?"

"I think you're looking at him."

"Holy shit."

"Exactly. Let me make a call." I dial the back door number for the office and enter Beth's extension.

"Full Service Brokers, Beth speaking."

"Hi, Beth. It's Watson. Bit of an emergency here."

"What is it?"

"By any chance did you go into my office on Friday, pull Massimo's commercial file and place coverage on his renewal on a whim?"

"What? No, of course not. Didn't you?"

"No. He just called me and—"

"When does it renew?" I hear her typing away on

her computer. "Oh, my God. Watson, it expired on Friday! Why are you asking? Has there been a claim?"

"Yes."

"Oh, my god! What are we going to do?"

"We gotta go to the big guy. Is he in, yet?"

"Yes, of course he's in. The sun's up, isn't it?"

"Nice. Okay, can you do me a really big favor?"

"You want me to break the news, right?"

"Just give him the basics. No coverage. Sewer back-up. Shop full of shit. Then get him to call me."

"You know he's going to kill you."

"Yes, I do. Thanks so much for this. I owe you big time."

"Bye, Watson," she says, and I believe I hear an air of finality in her voice. As if I might not be around to repay her. And I might not.

"So she didn't do it, either?" says Ray. "Who is she, your assistant?"

"Yes, kind of. But she mostly services my personal lines accounts. No, this one's on me. I am to blame. I've been so focused on this launch that everything else in my —"

Phone. That was quick. Ask not for whom the bell tolls. It tolls for me. "Hello, Watson Sinclair speaking."

"Hello, Watson. It's Don."

"Hi, Don. Sorry about all this."

"Don't talk. Listen." He's pretty calm. But as with Jess, I don't think it's a good sign. "Here's what we're going to do. Beth is going to call Service National and ask them to do the clean up and bill it to us. I am going to call the client and apologize on behalf of the brokerage and give him my personal assurance that he will be taken care of despite your monumental stupidity and laziness. I will take the entire cost of the clean up out of your commissions. You will be in my office in half an hour to discuss whether you still have a job. Good-bye."

Click.

Ray is looking at me for some reaction. "Well?"

"It went pretty well. He hasn't hired assassins to hunt me down and kill me."

"That well, huh?"

"Yeah. I'm going to be paying the whole bill."

"How much?"

"Who knows. Ten or twenty thousand, probably."

"Shit."

"The word of the day."

"Yuck."

"Yeah, I better go face my boss. I can't believe there's been no e-mails." I press the space bar to banish the screen saver so I can check Ray's laptop for any new developments and there is a new e-mail in the Inbox all of a sudden. The subject line just says "Question."

"Finally. Here's one from Gerald. He says, 'Ray, remember the time we went to Florida for sales conference and you and I went fishing together? What was the name of the fishing boat we chartered?' What the hell does that mean?"

I look over at Ray, but he is looking off down the hall somewhere. I'm getting a feeling about this that I don't like. Ray turns back to me with certainty in his eyes.

"He knows, Watson."

seventeen

"What do you mean, he knows?" I say, but I know, too. I just want to hear him say it.

"He knows I'm not at home and that there's something wrong. He has probably canned the launch."

"No." I can't believe what I'm hearing.

Ray finally looks at me. "Yes." He actually looks like he's broken up about this, too.

I lie back on the couch and close the laptop. "So it's over."

"Yes."

"What will they do instead, this late in the game?"

"It doesn't matter. Probably push the old favorites or just review the full roster."

It's all gone. The launch, my job, my marriage. Just like that. Is there anything else I can fuck up?

"I'm sorry, Watson. I was starting to believe you would pull the whole thing off."

"Yeah, so was I."

"So that's it, then."

"Yeah." My phone rings and I look at the display. Home—it's Jess. I almost don't have the energy to answer. But what the hell. "Hello?"

"Watson, the police are here." She's whispering forcefully. "They want to ask you questions about Ray Bennett. And someone is here from the FBI. What's this all about?"

I nod my head. The FBI. Of course. "I'm sorry about everything, Jess. I really am. You are the love of my life and always will be." I hang up and dial JC's phone. Ray is watching me and I think he has a pretty good idea what's going on, but he doesn't say anything.

"Watson. How's it going? Any news on the launch?" says JC in a rush.

"Abort. We're busted."

I hear him thinking it over. "Literally?"

"Yes. See you in ten minutes?"

His breath whistles against the phone. "Fuck me. Okay."

I hang up and walk into the guest room and quickly pack up my duffel bag and kit. There is an envelope in the drawer of the bedside table with $1000 in it. I put this in my duffel bag also. I grab the key from the dresser drawer and head back out to the den and undo Ray's leg chains. He rubs each ankle as the iron clasp comes off. I look him in the eye and find him smiling as I stand up.

"Ray, you are a comics god. I take my hat off to you. I'm sorry for all those things I posted about you on the Internet."

"Watson, it was a pleasure being your prisoner."

"You'll be okay getting home?"

"Don't worry about it."

"Excellent. Gotta run."

"Take care."

"You, too, buddy."

Ray gives me a hug, which is a surprise. I can feel he's lost weight from when I carried him in from the car a lifetime ago. That fat bastard is gone, replaced by this acerbic, hippy militant. He's a guy I'd like to know. Maybe I can correspond with him someday. From prison. I head for the stairs and up towards the front hall with Ray following. I put on my coat, open the door and step out, only to see my parents getting out of their car. My dad is pulling a monster stretch when he sees me, just as Ray emerges, blinking, into the light of day. Perfect.

"Watson? What's going on?" says my Dad.

"Mom! Dad!" I call out. "Welcome home!" Hysterical.

My mother comes around the front of the car and looks at Ray and then me. "What is all this about you moving out of your home? Are you and Jessica having problems?"

My dad looks at Ray. "Marnie, maybe this could wait until we're inside."

Motioning towards him, I say. "Mom, Dad... this is my friend Ray Bennett. Ray, this is George Sinclair and this is Marnie Sinclair."

I smile back and forth and they all look at me like I'm crazy. Then they shake hands and exchange pleasantries while the remnants of my composure and, who knows?, maybe my sanity, collapse inside me. I can feel a cascade of horror beginning in my throat and stiffening the muscle groups all the way down to my stomach, which is twisted in knots. I feel incapable of tears, even. The light is so bright out here, even with the sodden clumps of grass peeking out from here and there in the snow, the wet brick of their house drying in patches. It all seems so hyper-real.

"What's this all about?" says my Dad. All three of them are just standing there, looking at me. Whatever disappointment I've been in the past will soon double and double again.

"Mom, Dad... I love you guys and I'd normally be

happy to stay and chat, but I've gotta get the fuck outta Dodge."

"Language, Watson," says my Mom, as if swearing is the worst thing a person could be accused of. It's a kind of innocence which all by itself puts a constriction on my chest. I try to fight through it for a deep breath and walk towards my car with her stern glare still on my back. I throw my duffel in the back seat and close the door. Unthinkingly, I start the car and put it in gear. I wave to them as I pull out of the driveway and poor Mom and Dad are just standing there with their jaws hanging open. Ray waves, which is a nice gesture. I don't envy him all the explanations he'll have to make, but I know I couldn't bear to hear them, even if I weren't being pursued by the police.

And as I am thinking about being caught, I realize that a criminal conviction would mean I would lose my RIBO license, never mind my job. I have lost my livelihood and my freedom in one stupid, stupid act of desperation. I always wondered what my legacy on this earth would be and this is it. A fuck up. A criminal. No comic strip collections preserved for the ages. No wife. No family. Nothing. I feel like puking and then driving my car into a tree, but something makes me keep going.

As I am making the turn on Ridout towards downtown, I see a police car in the distance driving along Commissioners Road towards my parents' house. I'm driving away and I watch in my rearview mirror as the cop passes through the intersection behind me, followed by an ominous looking black sedan. The Feds. It's an international incident! My life is about to become a cautionary tale and a bad Internet rumor all in the same day.

@watsonsinclair
Watson Sinclair

Tweeps: unexpected calamity. Project...
delayed. Will be unavailable for awhile.
Thanks for all the love. #wishmeluck

7 minutes ago via web ☆ Favorite ↩ Reply 🗑 Delete

eighteen

I've never been to Saskatchewan. Thirty-three years in Canada and I never got the urge. But with their booming oil and gas, potash mining and agricultural economy, it's a great place to look for cash-paying, anonymous Joe jobs and stay hidden. Lots of people coming from out of province looking for work, new communities springing up close to the mines—it's all hustle and bustle and no one will take much notice of a couple of new guys. Unless a Canada-wide manhunt breaks out on CBC News and they start searching every gas station, residence, warehouse, pool house, outhouse and gingerbread house looking for fugitives. That would be bad.

We had always planned for an exit strategy, hoping we'd never have to use it. We planned everything on this kidnapping, right down to the best way to get Ray to give up the passwords. Waterboarding was going to be our ultimate tactic if nothing else worked. Lots of videos on that available on YouTube. It sickens me when I think about it, because I now know there is a big difference between watching a video of something happening and being a part of it yourself.

We knew that kidnapping and torture would mean jail time, so we always intended to run if it looked like we were going to get caught. I drive downtown thinking all this and imagining the sound of sirens around every corner. The cinnamon bun is like a brick in my stomach and I feel both a need for more caffeine and a sense that I've had way too much. I'm jittery and on the verge of tears. I alternate shallow breathing with sucking in wind like I just came up out of the water, heart thudding, fingers gripping the steering wheel like a lifeline. I don't know how we're ever going to get to Saskatchewan, but one thing at a time, I guess.

The sight of JC standing in front of the Central Library with his hiking pack, watching each car pass with sick concern in his eyes, his mouth half open like he's dazed, brings a sob from my chest that I choke down. I pull the car over to the curb and put it in 'Park' with the flashers on. I pop the trunk and get out to help him with his pack. He lets me take it off his back and stuff it in the trunk and he just stands there for a second, looking down, standing in a puddle of dirty slush.

"This sucks, buddy," I say. "But we gotta go."

I nudge his shoulder in the direction of the passenger side and it starts him walking toward the car and we both get in at the same time.

"Which way to the 401?" I say as I put the car in gear.

"Go Hamilton Road out to Highbury. It's fastest."

"Okay." I drive the half block to Wellington and then turn right towards our exit route.

"So what happened?" JC sighs as if he doesn't want to ask this and doesn't want to hear the answer. Some questions are like that.

"Everything at once," I say and then I hold my breath as we pull up to a red light at York Street. A cop is waiting at the light to turn left onto Wellington. We are second in line in the left lane behind a red Ford minivan, perpendicular to him, so the cop can see us if he looks over here. I look over and JC locks eyes with me and nods. I grit my teeth and smile. "Do you think they have an APB out on my Honda?"

"A very normal conversation is what we're having," says JC. He breaks into a very normal, not-nervous laugh. "If they do, we're toast."

The cop switches on his lights, turns left and accelerates away down Wellington. We both catch a large breath.

"Do you think he saw us?" says JC.

"Don't know. If the cops are still at my parents' house talking to Ray, maybe they haven't put a notice out, yet. With the FBI involved, I'm pretty sure they will."

"The what did you say?"

"Oh, yeah. The FBI knocked on my door first thing this morning with some cops, asking about Ray. Jess called me at my parents' place to let me know. We are busted wide open and gutted. And by the way, Gerald figured out the whole thing and probably ratted us out. The launch is canned and just for good measure, a big claim blew up on me at work and it looks like I'm out of a job. How was your morning?"

"*Calisse ferme ta gueule. Merde.* So Jess called you on your cell? Where is it now?"

"I sent one last Twitter update and then broke it into pieces and threw each bit out the window in a different set of bushes on my way downtown. Yours?"

"The garbage at Little Red Roaster."

"You didn't get a coffee?"

"Already drank it."

"Huh. I could go for another coffee."

"Yeah."

Our light turns green and we proceed through the intersection, under the railway overpass. We turn left down Hamilton. I am hardly concentrating on driving because I am so conscious of watching out for cops. I'm looking in parking lots, down side streets and side driveways and I have to punch the brakes hard to avoid rear-ending the car in front of me when the light turns at Colborne and I don't notice. JC is jerked forward into his seat belt.

"You watch the road," he says. "I'll watch for cops."

"Okay," I say. "Good idea." I relax my grip on the steering wheel and try for a deep breath. I need to calm down with some yoga breathing. It's amazing how often that shit comes in handy. I breathe in the silence and breathe out the noise. When the light turns, I just go with the flow along Hamilton Road.

"So the launch is canned for sure?" says JC.

I nod and take in another life-preserving breath which is working wonders with my erratic heartbeat.

He looks at his watch. It's 9:24 on the dashboard clock. "But the sales conference is going on right now. What are they going to go with instead?"

I sigh. "I asked that, too. Ray figured they'd probably push the old favorites or just review the whole line-up. They have sales materials for that kind of stuff made up and ready to go just in case they can't get a new feature ready in time. Or their editor-in-chief gets kidnapped."

"Right. Of course. Good thinking."

"Sure."

"So the FBI is at your parent's house along with the cops. City cops or OPP?"

"City cops. I saw the cars coming up

Commissioners as I was making my escape."

"I wonder how the jurisdiction thing works."

"No idea. I know I don't want to be caught by any of them."

"Right. Me neither."

We're both silent now as JC checks the side streets and parking lots so favored by traffic cops. I keep my eyes on the road and contemplate this new life on the run, where this will be our new norm. We'll always be like this, looking over a shoulder going around every street corner, wondering which face is going to brighten when it sees us because that person has recognized our pictures from some newspaper article. Will there be newspaper articles? How fast can we grow beards? Will they sell hair dye at the bus station? What the fuck were we thinking?

We make it to Highbury without incident and turn south towards the 401, slouching down in our seats, eyes still flicking every which way, twitchy and nervous as hunted animals.

nineteen

It's 10:00 by the time we get to Woodstock, a town named for a bird in a comic strip. You'd think there would be a bust of Sparky Schultz in the center of town, but nothing. I think the City Council here is way tight-fisted. But of course they have plenty of money to shell out for a major Community Center and Sports Complex in the new part of town with gymnasia, arenas, meeting rooms, a college and tons of free parking, which is where we drop off the Honda. It's a busy place with people coming and going at all hours. The south side of the arena is at the back with no entrances, so not much pedestrian traffic and there are no street lights over here. It will be a good quiet spot to park for the long term. Until we are long gone.

We walk across the parking lot. I'm glad I have the waterproof jacket for this weather, but this is still February in Canada and we're heading north. This jacket will be useless after tomorrow. The sky is gray, the snow is a dirty white and the street is covered with sand and salt.

We know enough not to use our cars or credit cards and to not phone our spouses from wherever we land. E-mail should be all right. It will be old-fashioned, like John Dillinger on the lam, sending love letters to his little woman. We grab our bags out of my trunk and then close and lock the car. I keep the keys just to have them. I can't figure any percentage in throwing them away versus being caught with them. Caught is caught, I figure. It is still drizzling and mild enough, but I zip up my Gore-Tex parka and pull up my hood. The slowly-dissolving snowbanks look sodden and forlorn. More water for the sewer system. I wonder how Massimo is making out at the shop. Donald has probably called him by now and got everything underway. What a responsible guy. He always knows what to do.

"It's cold," says JC. "This will all freeze into some nasty conditions."

"I'm sure everything will look different once we get north of Toronto," I say. "They probably haven't had any rain or melting and it's just winter as usual for them."

"Yeah. Great."

It's about a two kilometer trudge from the Community Center to the TA Travel Center, which is a truck stop out by the 401 and the Sweaburg Road Exit. We stay on Finkle Street all the way to the end, retracing the path we followed in the car, which didn't seem this long when we were driving it. Now that I'm carrying a heavy duffel bag and getting wet it seems like a very long walk indeed. Lots of houses under construction in this area. Guys swinging hammers and carting drywall around. A guy up on a roof laying out some roof shingles. I wonder if some of them take cash under the table and work under an assumed name and drink up their pay every night to try to dull the hurt and the mistakes and the regrets.

At the end of Finkle, we turn right on Athlone Avenue, which is named for a town in the center of Ireland that I've heard my parents talk about. It's on the road from Dublin to Galway. I wonder how they're getting along with the police and the FBI. I hope Mom doesn't tell them about the swearing. What's that you say, Mrs. Sinclair? We need to add a count of Felonious Imprecation on top of everything else? This guy's going up on the website. 'Canada's Most Wanted Kidnapper, Torturer and Potty Mouth.'

When we get to Mill Street, we turn left and we can see the TA sign, which is a relief because we can get ourselves inside and dry off. It also prompts a deep sigh because I am reminded this is just the first stop on a long and tiring journey with an uncertain outcome. That's its own kind of exhausting. JC's spirits must be as damp as the bottom of his wrinkle-free cotton Dockers because he isn't saying jack shit. I guess I don't know what to say either. Do we apologize to each other for coming up with and executing a monumentally stupid plan? I hope he doesn't think all this was more my idea than his.

It's almost 10:30 as we're walking in the front door of the truck stop. We stop to check the Greyhound schedule: the next bus to Toronto is at 11:30, which is perfect. We put our hoods down and shake off a bit. To our left is a buffet restaurant which smells like a lot of deep fried things facing off against a lot of fried meats to see who gets to stop a trucker's heart on the road to Tennessee. For some reason there are pay phones at every table. Weird. To our right is a variety store and straight ahead are the washrooms, but also, bizarrely, a sign saying there is a barber shop, travel service, a Chiropractor's office, a paralegal, movie theater, video arcade, some showers, full laundry and a chapel. I could totally live here. But for now, I need the bathroom most of all. I scan all the people, looking for uniforms. Luckily there is no donut shop here.

"Washroom break?" I say to JC, who is also surveying our surroundings suspiciously.

"Yeah, definitely," he says. "How do we not look like two guys who look like our descriptions? Can we do

198

that easily?"

We start in the direction of the washroom. "I was thinking about that. I could use a new coat, anyway, so that's a start. Is there a thrift shop near the Toronto bus station?"

"I don't know," says JC. "I wondered more about our hair and stuff."

We reach the urinals and unzip, keeping our packs on our backs with a one urinal cushion between us. "Well, I could grow a beard and you could shave yours, I guess. You'll need to cut all your hair off. We can keep our eyes open for hair dye. One of us can go lighter and one can go darker. That's a timeworn classic. Anything else?"

"What about an eye patch or a crutch or something?"

"Yes! And a parrot for your shoulder and a bottle of Captain Morgan in your hook hand? 'Aar, ya filthy coppers. Ye'll never take me alive.'"

He laughs. We zip up, flush and move over to wash our hands.

"Let's check what the variety store has to offer," I say. We look at ourselves in the mirror and we don't look as terrified as I feel. JC holds his hair back on both sides like he was going to put it in a ponytail.

"I haven't had short hair since high school," he says.

I nod and move over to dry my hands. I'll give him a moment.

After another couple of seconds of gazing and self love, he sighs and comes over to the hand dryer. "Long, beautiful hair is probably not the best thing to have in prison, anyway," he says.

"Hey, enough of that talk. We're okay so far. No fatalism until you see a flashing cherry light and cops closing in on us with their guns drawn."

"Fair enough."

We walk out into the hallway and wander down to see the movie theaters and offices and what not. It's like a tiny world back there. The offices and two chair barbershop are behind glass doors and we can see two fat guys with beards getting their hair cut. The movie theater is a smallish room with 30 or 40 seats facing either a very small movie screen or very large TV screen. Religious pamphlets are posted just everywhere at the back and by the washrooms and there's a phone which purports to be a prayer line for truckers. The Almighty on direct dial.

I pick up a pamphlet and show it to JC. "I guess it's really important that truckers have God as their co-pilot in case Jesus has to take the wheel on the road to Georgia due to a massive myocardial infarction. 'You take it from here, Jesus, good buddy. There's some money for the tolls on the dash there. Urrrkkklll.'"

He laughs at this one, but not for long and the smile fades quickly into a tight-lipped, telescopic stare as he puts the pamphlet in his back pocket. Damn French Catholic upbringing. Now he's looking all serious and he's probably thinking how God is looking down from the pearly clouds or whatever and judging his ass, so I steer him towards the variety store.

"Let's check for that hair dye," I say to him and he nods.

The store here is actually a hybrid, or tri-brid, between small grocery store, truck accessories and coffee shop. Everything your road weary traveler or trucker might want, including an impressive glass knick-knack cabinet for guys who forgot their anniversaries and are on their way home to dodgy situations, I guess. There are all sorts of gifts, DVD movies, keychains, souvenirs of Canada, stuffed animals (in case you forgot your kid's birthday) and a small rack of greeting cards. The grocery section includes your basic canned and packaged crap, an enormous display of energy bars, more caffeinated cold beverages than I've ever imagined, chocolate and chips and whatnot, travel laundry supplies and toiletries of every description. Except hair dye. The only thing they have that's close is peroxide.

"I guess our hair will have to wait," says JC. He looks relieved.

"Your flowing locks live to stir poetically in another breeze," I say. "I'm getting a coffee. Do you want one?"

"Sure."

We get our coffees and head outside to wait. The cold drizzle dulls the ache in my throat from all my forced cheerfulness. It feels like the beginnings of strep throat. All my regrets are on a continuous loop and the time seems to pass in its own abstract way so I don't even notice when the Greyhound bus pulls up in the parking lot.

"Watson," says JC, pulling my arm. "The bus is here. We've got to go."

I stumble across the slushy parking lot, following JC and we line up behind a couple of young girls with no luggage. The bus driver takes our bags and stows them in the compartment at the bottom, we pay him in nice, anonymous, untraceable cash money and we are on our way to Toronto. The bus door hisses closed behind us and we look down a long row of upturned faces and suspicious, searching eyes. Or is that my paranoia kicking in?

twenty

Toronto, Ontario: the Big Smoke. "Toronto the Good." Hogtown. *Trawnna* to the locals. Home of the Maple Laughs. T-dot, Hollywood North, the GTA, the 416... to us it's just a bus transfer point.

Our Woodstock bus lets us off at about 1:15 in a smaller bus terminal building behind the main building at Bay and Dundas and we all mill around until the driver opens the swing-up doors underneath the bus and passes out all the suitcases and boxes and strange-looking bags of sports equipment. We have to cross Elizabeth Street to get to the main terminal where we can buy our tickets to freedom. Freedom, Saskatchewan. Sounds like a CBC sitcom. We walk through a long corridor full of rows of silver lockers along the wall to our right and a line of square windows looking out on the lineups on the main bus platforms to our left. There's a crowd trudging along in little groups of ones, twos and threes, mostly students.

The sliding doors open onto the lobby of the historic two-story Toronto Coach Terminal building. There is an escalator to our right which leads down to the underground Path and the Dundas Subway Station. We cross the floor of a large waiting area which looks like a departure gate in an airport with lots of bored people sitting around in rows of green plastic seats. This area is surrounded by glass walls which look out onto the comings and goings of a fleet of buses.

Across from "Kramden's Kafé," there is a corral system of poles and red extendable strips which herd people towards the ticket counter. As it is not very busy right now, those of use who are looking to purchase tickets to continue our journeys just follow the maze back and forth, turning and retracing our steps till we get to the end. JC and I are third in line and it only takes a few minutes before one of the helpful, bored-looking ticket sellers is waving us up to her wicket. She is black with dark skin and her hair tied back in thin braids. She's rather portly and wearing the same unflattering light blue shirt as all the other ticket sellers, sitting on a tall chair in front of her computer terminal. We walk up together.

"Where you boys headed?" she says to us.

"We need to get to Saskatchewan," says JC. "Saskatoon, let's say." He says this almost apologetically and waits for her to tell him this is the craziest plan she's ever heard. Instead she just nods and types away on her keyboard, watching her monitor for answers.

"It's $210 one way," she says at last. "You get on the 4:00 bus to Sudbury, boarding at platform 11. Be there 15 minutes early."

"We'll take one each," says JC. I nod and concentrate on not crying.

* * *

We step outside into the gray light and gray slush of this dismal February day. Every time I think I'm getting used to my situation, something new will come along to make it feel real all over again. Buying bus tickets to a place far away from Jessica is the last thing I thought I'd ever do. I look at JC's face, which is as grim as I expect mine is looking right now.

We have a couple of hours to kill. We take a look at our surroundings, and right there, three doors from the bus terminal, is a barber shop. I look at JC and laugh.

"Looks like it's time, buddy," I say.

He looks fearful. "What about the hair dye?"

I point over at the next store, which is the Toronto Barber & Beauty Supply. "Yeah, we've got that covered, too."

"Oh," he says. He's looking more queasy.

"You want to check for the hair dye first?"

"Sure."

I look at my watch as we trudge over to the store, not in any kind of hurry. It's not even 1:45. Still two hours before we can board the bus. It feels weird not to be getting texts or phone calls. I wonder what Jess is doing right now. Mom? Ray? I feel like a penguin who jumped on the wrong bit of ice and just broke it off and floated away from home. Okay, yes, with my best friend penguin, but he's turned into a mope who's way too feather proud right now. I take a look up and down Dundas for cops before I open the door and walk into a store full of hair supplies.

We wander up and down the aisles long enough and we find a dizzying array of color choices: Chestnut Brown, Light Ash Brown, Champagne Blond, Light Butterscotch, Honeyed Amber, Rich Auburn, Fox Red, Strawberry Blond, Jet black... it is so hard to guess the perfect shade for working in the potash mine in Moose Jaw, Saskatchewan.

"So, what do you think?" I say. JC is reading the side of the box of some color or other. "I think the accepted convention for those 'on the lam' is to find a gas station bathroom and color our hair in the sink."

He nods and puts the box back on the shelf.

"Okay," I say. "So you're not ready for that, yet. Let's get a couple of boxes for later and get our haircuts first." I pick up a box of light blond and dark brown at random and walk over to the counter to pay.

"Wait," he says. "Which one of those is for you and which is for me?"

I get a couple of twenties out of my wallet. "I don't care. You choose."

"Good, because I'm not going blond."

"That's cool, because I'll be having more fun."

I get my change and put the bag of hair color in my duffel bag and we are out of there. JC suggests we turn down Dundas and see what's down that way, but I think he is more interested in what is not down that way, namely a Barber Shop. That's cool, I guess. I'm trying to imagine the odds that cops are already scrambled with our photos here in Toronto. It's not like we're murderers or child kidnappers who still have our abductee with us. Would they really scramble a province-wide manhunt for a couple of cartoonists who effectively used extreme measures to seek a promotion from their boss? It's almost like a white collar crime, when I think of it that way. A workplace dispute.

So we walk along Dundas towards the back end of the bus station, me in my happy cloud of delusion, passing a couple of restaurants, a nail shop and another Barber Shop that JC pretends not to notice, looking up at the sky and swiveling around to look across the street instead, where there is yet another fucking Barber Shop. JC has stopped walking and I know he sees it, too.

"What's with all the haircut options, am I right?" I say. Somewhere a siren sounds but I can't tell if it's moving away from us or getting closer. I pat him on the shoulder. "Are you ready to do this, partner?"

twenty-one

"*Sacré crisse,*" says JC, ducking down in his seat. "*Les boeufs.*"

I look over his shoulder to see out the bus window. "Cows? Where?"

"No, cops." He motions his thumb towards the Barrie Greyhound bus station as we are passing by the front of the building and I see it. A police station, right in the frickin' terminal. What are the odds? Worse, what are the odds that our mugshots are popping up on their monitors or printing off on their fax machine right now?

"Sacred Christ is right," I say, also sliding down in my seat because it feels like the right thing to do. "On a bicycle."

I look at JC, who is looking worried and pathetic with all his hair chopped off, sporting a conservative new side-parted hairstyle. I can't take him seriously. Out the front window of the bus I can see water and then we are turning right to circle around behind the bus station. The view of the bay from here is spectacular and I'm reminded of how beautiful this place is in better times. We hear the crackle of the bus driver switching on the PA.

"Ladies and gentlemen, welcome to Barrie. It is now 5:30. If you are going farther north, the same coach will be leaving north in one hour. 6:30, same coach, same spot. Thank-you for traveling Greyhound."

We pull to a stop behind the terminal building next to a green metal shelter the length of the bus. The sidewalks have been shoveled, but there is a good covering of snow everywhere, so we are definitely getting closer to the Great White North. People are gathering their things and getting off the bus and groups of shivering people stand around outside, some smoking, some just standing under other bus shelters, awaiting salvation. No police officer scans the crowds, bopping a nightstick against the palm of one hand or holding a photo up to the light. I look at JC. He is pulling at the wisps of hair behind his ears and looking shorn and pathetic, like a dog just home from the groomer. Wait till he gets his Chocolate Mahogany on.

He looks at me and says, "Let's just leave the bags and not even go inside. We'll walk across the street to the Thrift Store like we know what we're doing and haven't got a care in the world. No looking around like we're worried, okay?"

"Okay," I say, glancing around worriedly.

We walk down the center aisle of the bus, which is now almost empty, except for a couple of people sleeping. JC steps down onto the sidewalk and I follow him. He is walking across the platform like a roadie for a bebop group in the 40's, so I fall in beside him matching his groove, shoulders rocking with each long stride. He said not to have a care in the world. He looks at me and laughs, so I laugh, too, but I'm just doing it to look normal, not because I think it's funny. I'm too aware that we're passing right by the Police Station window and I really want to see if there is someone looking out, but I manage to resist the urge.

We pass under another long green metal bus shelter on a concrete island between two bus lanes and then we are crossing over Maple Avenue towards the Thrift Store.

The last thing I said to JC before he noticed the police station was, "Hey, look. There's a Salvation Army right across from the bus station. How convenient is that?" And that is pretty amazing luck, when you think about it, so it's obvious to me now that for every piece of good luck there is an equal and opposite piece of bad luck about to happen. These are the forces at work in the universe, keeping things in balance. I wonder about all the bad luck I have had recently with no good luck to balance it out, though. Maybe Isaac Newton had it wrong.

When we have bebopped our way through the parking lot without a care in the world or a nervous glance over our shoulders, we find ourselves, for the second time in a week counting our shopping spree for Ray, in a Thrift Store. Our new reality for the next how many years? Following the signs to the men's clothing section, I look for coats and see there is a rack of a bunch of them against the wall. This is pretty small compared to the one in London. The smell of this place is like every Goodwill or Sally Ann I've ever been in, like a college student's apartment or sticking your head right into a laundry hamper. You could blindfold me and walk me into any one of these stores and I'd instantly know where I was by sense of smell alone.

The pickings are fairly slim, especially in my size. My dream coat for my flight from justice was either a thick red and black lumberjacket, a classic of the Canadian North, or a Navy Pea Coat with a black dockworkers cap, but I am out of luck on both counts. The fashion in Barrie seems to be polyester, poly-filled zip front bomber jackets with multi-hued swatches of material emblazoned over the arms and front in haphazard bits and pieces. They must have a Walmart here.

I pick one with navy, purple and red and take it

over to the cash register to pay. JC is over looking at the books like he might actually buy a couple. Because "Flowers in the Attic" by V.C. Andrews is a timeless classic. I pay the nice Native woman the twenty bucks for the coat. I get her to cut the tag off and I just put it on over my Gore-Tex mountain parka. It sticks out at the bottom a little bit, but it's not too bad. Between the two of them and a good sweater, I should be able to get by.

"Hey, buddy," I say to JC. "You finding anything good over there?"

"No," he says. "You ready?"

"Yep."

I hold open the door and he joins me on the sidewalk. The Salvation Army building is sandwiched between two older-looking apartment buildings. We follow the walkway between the parking lots back to Maple Street and we can see Dunlop Street and also the bus station from here. I check my watch.

"We have 50 minutes left to get back on the bus," I say. "D'you want to get a bite to eat?"

JC shrugs, still looking towards the bus station.

"We probably shouldn't eat in the terminal building, just to be safe." I nudge him on the shoulder and point towards Dunlop Street where we came in on the bus. "C'mon. I noticed a 'Pharaoh's Pita' back this way."

"Okay," says JC.

The sidewalk on this side street stretches back towards the busy road, icy in patches and bare cement in others, and it seems like it is so far to walk. I'm no longer cold in my double coat, but I'm so tired. I look at JC and register the same look of fatigue, like we could eat, could get back on the bus and continue our escape, live on in the Prairie world of wheat and potash mining, or we could just call it quits right now and take the jail time in exchange for a really good night's sleep and not having to worry anymore.

It's probably only a block to the Pita place, but as a part of our overall journey, it seems impassable.

twenty-two

JC and I are on the bus a mile north of Barrie
heading for our transfer in northern Ontario. Not doing
much talking. I realize now I never asked JC how he broke
the news to Sylvie. Did he tell her in person or wait till she
left, packing his things and phoning her with the news?
How did she react? How does their love manifest when
the chips are down, I wonder? At least his wife didn't
abandon him over a few late nights and a missed date.
Whatever happened to for better or for worse? Oh, yeah.
It's refusing to die, resurrecting itself in reruns which take
up a lot of precious real estate on the comics pages,
preventing new artists like ourselves from making a go of
it. I'm sorry your husband left you, Lynn Johnston, but it's
time to move on. Are you listening, Garry Trudeau? What
about all you second generation cartoonists on bullshit
strips like *Hi and Lois* and "Hagar the Self-Descriptive?"
Ya heard? *Peanuts* re-runs? How long ago did Charles
Schulz die, anyway?

Beetle Bailey can give the Sarge one more rim job
and then be gone. The military was out after the first Gulf
War, for god's sake. I don't know how they got past
Vietnam with that lame shit. Turn the lights out when you
leave, *Blondie*. You, too, *Garfield*. 1600 "I hate Monday"
jokes are enough, I think. It's time for some new blood on
the Comics page and if a little blood has to be spilled to get
it done, I'm not squeamish. There are five more syndicates

out there. We're coming for you: notice has been served.

Bill Watterson knew the score. So did Gary Larson and Berke Breathed. Those guys got it right. Every great new strip that has come along got its shot because some older, popular strip stepped aside, leaving space for the new generation. But not many have followed in their footsteps, whether it was due to the greedy syndicates keeping it going to protect their turf, or the artists themselves not knowing when to retire. It was this kind of shit that got us worked up in the first place. Stewing over the closed economic system that tries to keep a brother down. Cursing Ray over and over for his lack of response on our development concept. We were so close we could taste it, but we just couldn't break in.

It was there that the plan was formed. First over beer and misery, then scotch and seething, and finally, pure venom. After the slow burn of so many months of frustration and a certain number of drinks, we were willing to consider anything to make the thing happen. I'm sure alcohol consumption in general (and Glenfiddich's 12-year-old single malt in particular) has lead to worse plans, but this one was our worst. Now that our lives are ruined, we know this for sure. But at the time it seemed like a brilliant idea. We thought if we planned out every detail, we couldn't fail.

The idea itself came from an offhand script idea I had written down on one of the index cards we were exchanging back when we were building up our fury at Ray. I have it with me still. I pull it out of my pocket to look at it.

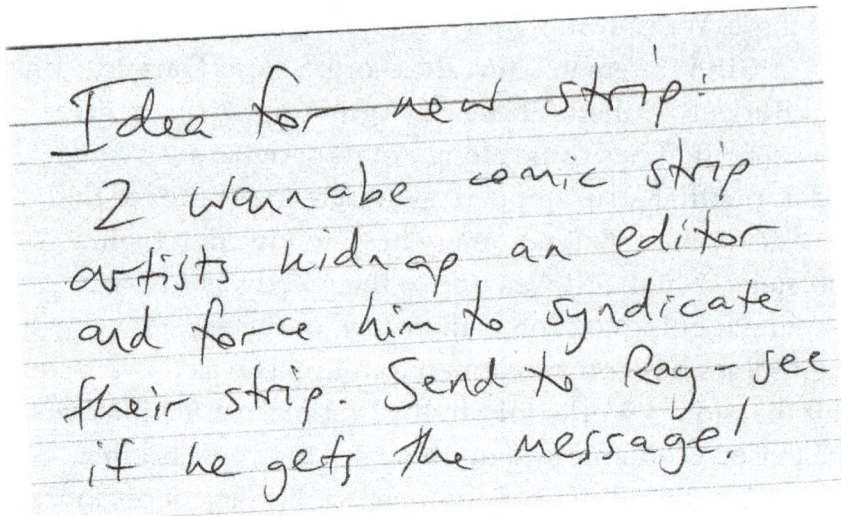

Idea for new strip:
2 wannabe comic strip artists kidnap an editor and force him to syndicate their strip. Send to Ray — see if he gets the message!

JC looks at the index card and snorts. "And here my troubles began."

"You're not wrong," I say, sighing.

I look at the card. Just words on paper. A few swirls of ink on a bit of dead tree. What alchemy brings the two substances together and creates the magic that leads to action, to change in one's life, to purpose and determination? It's laughable. But that same bit of pigment rubbed up against some bolts of newsprint is what all this was about. A desire to see the magic every day that puts thoughts and images into ink and paper and moves them through many hands and into many lives we'll never understand or know about. Our creation.

But creation is not enough or why wouldn't we just take a strip and hammer it up on a telephone pole and be done with it? Appreciation is not enough or why wouldn't we just print a bunch of strips and distribute them to our friends and family for their enjoyment? Or even post it on a blog or webportal and enjoy the approving comments posted by comixgeek82 and slinkyboy. The trouble was the yardstick we came to understand as the proof of having made it in this world of comics, this strange intersection of art and commerce, where the artist and the capitalist move forward together with a joint venture. *We think we've got something here, world. You take a look and let us know what you think.*

I put the card back into my pocket. I can't bring myself to tear it up, yet. I'd sleep if I could. But regret has its own momentum. Apparently, there are things I need to work through before exhaustion can overtake my adrenal system. Oh, well. It's a long ride to Saskatoon. I'll have lots of time for sleep. Lots of time for Jessica to give me hell in my dreams. She would have a thing or two to say about this screw up, that's for sure. *Yes, dear. I shouldn't have kidnapped the nice Editor. Yes, I should have talked to you about it first. I'm sorry.*

"What about my Sylvie?" says JC. His arms are crossed over his belly like he's feeling sick.

"I was just thinking the same thing," I say. "About my Jess."

"She sounded so confused and pissed off and then scared. How can I just leave it like that?"

"We'll hit an Internet café in Saskatoon and send long e-mails to the wives explaining everything."

"I can't do it."

"Well, I'll help you. We can just copy and paste, probably."

"No, I mean I can't just not see her for whatever months or years we'll have to be away. I'll miss her too much. I don't think I can live without her."

"Buddy, you'll have me."

He looks at me, the despondence giving way to incredulity. "I've got to give myself up. Surrender to the cops."

"But then you'll just go to jail and not see her there, either."

"I know, but at least I'll get conjugal visits."

"No, I think that's only for lifers."

"No way."

"I don't know, maybe. But isn't freedom worth it in the end? You can correspond by e-mail and then you can make plans to change your identities and move to a new city when the heat dies down. Stick to the plan."

"But how long will that take? The fucking FBI is involved. Do you think they'll just let it go? What if they want to try us in New York?"

"I don't know. I couldn't believe they actually showed up at my house. I thought they'd have to go through the RCMP or something."

JC nods. "Yeah, yeah. For sure. And how did they know to go to your house?"

"I've been thinking about that and I realized something. When I went home on Friday, I was checking for voice mail on Ray's cell phone and then I changed jackets because it was raining out. I must have left it there in my winter coat and maybe they tracked it by GPS."

"That makes sense. Son of a bitch. I'm glad you didn't have it at your parents' house, then, or they'd have been knocking on their front door instead and we'd be cooling our heels in jail right now."

"You see? It's a nice feeling to be free."

"I guess so." He rests his head on the seat back and closes his eyes, then opens them again and digs in his backpack for his iPod. He plugs in his ear buds and I hear the far off sound of Neil Diamond crooning in a tiny, tiny voice. Really? Turn On Your Heartlight? Dude has never had any taste in music. But he is good at sending unspoken messages. I'm guessing he doesn't want to talk anymore.

This talk of conjugal visits is unsettling. I can't stop thinking about her. All the little things I have come to know about her. The way she cuddles up to me on the couch when we're watching a movie. The way she flips her hair behind one ear when she's making an important point. The way she eats fruit with a knife — never biting into it, just cutting off little pieces and placing them on her tongue gingerly from the flat of the blade. The cheesy sci-fi novels she is always reading. Her secret smiles. Her openness. The way she hums when she is blowing me, because of some article she read in Cosmo. Adorable.

I wonder will a week ago Sunday be the last time I have sex for a month? A year? A decade? Or will I have to move on with my life and find someone else? Jess said it might be over, then I left, now I've really left… maybe I'll have to become a bigamist with an unsuspecting second wife up in Frontiertown. Maybe the local barmaid will have me and I will spin tall tales about an imaginary life before she knew me and we will sit on the balcony of our second floor apartment above the local saloon and watch the drunks come and go on her nights off. I should do all right. What woman doesn't love a drifter with a sketchy past?

I don't care. I'll get by even if I have to pay toothless hookers for handjobs out behind the woodshed. I'm picturing a lot of woodsheds in Saskatchewan, for some reason. And woodstoves. We're not going to let this drag us down. And we're going ahead with this strip no matter what. We've got too much material to kill it now. We can go to Internet cafés and libraries and post the damn thing on a webcomic portal after all. I'll tweet about our defiant struggle and spread the word as @watsonsinclair on twitter. We'll become a cyberspace legend: the guys who kidnapped Ray Bennett and went on the lam, putting out an underground comic strip by themselves. Rebels to the end! Never buckling under the pressure, always one step ahead of the law. Sticking it to the corporate weasels from hiding.

We can post blog entries about what we think about the comics industry. Tear the motherfucker down one brick at a time. I've got plenty of opinions. There will be such a public outcry that we will be the most popular online comic strip since PVP and Penny Arcade. Ray will drop all charges just so we'll sign with them. And if not him, then one of the other five syndicates. They'll all get a copy and the highest bidder will win. Even Ray won't just skate by on our friendship. He'll have to pony up like everyone else. And no development deals! Straight to syndication only. We're developed enough.

And if they don't give us the R-E-S-P-E-C-T, well, I know a great recipe for chloroform and I still have some of those roofies left. Not that much of a stretch. We've had a practice run, so we know the mistakes we'll have to fix. It doesn't—

"What are you thinking about?" says JC, removing an earbud.

"What?" I say.

"You've got a weird look on your face. Like you're planning to burn down your school or something."

"I was just—"

"Well, stop it. No more evil plots. Go to sleep."

And, as if I've finally been given permission, I do just that.

I wake up in darkness as the bus slows and stops for a traffic light. Not many of those up here in the north country, so we must be coming to a town. I was dreaming of Donald Gill giving me shit for being late for work, except he was wearing shorts and a T-shirt and I couldn't figure out if it was casual day and I forgot. Our next transfer is in Sudbury and then Sault Ste. Marie. We'll be on the bus all night and I'm already uncomfortable from sleeping sitting up. I stretch and take a look out the window. We're in a town, pulling in across from a Staples and a Leon's, so I'm guessing it must be Sudbury, because we already passed through Parry Sound. The bus station is an L-shaped gray building and we are stopping to the left side of the long section which points to the road, alongside another bus.

I look at my watch. It's quarter past nine. The day is almost over, thank god.

"Ladies and gentlemen, we are now approaching the Sudbury station. If you are continuing on to another destination, you will have to get off and transfer to another bus. If this is your last stop, welcome to Sudbury."

I look over at JC and he is still awake, still listening to his iPod. He looks pretty miserable. I pull an earbud out of his ear and he finally looks at me.

"Time to snap out of it, buddy," I say to him. "Tomorrow's a new day and we're alive and free and ready to start our new lives."

"Grun-gra," he says.

"Good point. That was grumblicious and I know

how you feel. It sucks to be here and not home in our own beds, snuggling up to our wives waiting to hear how our comic strip launch is going. But we're here and we might as well make the best of it. Let's do this well, find a good situation, keep our ears to the ground, listen for opportunities and move forward with our plan."

"Bah," he says, turning his head to look at the Sudbury bus station as everybody is getting up to gather their things.

"No, no. Just think about it. The better we are at this, the better our chances at figuring out a way back to where we want to be. Short term pain, long term gain. They can't keep surveillance on the wives forever, right?"

He looks at me hopefully.

"Now you feel me? They have this thing in Saskatoon called the University of Saskatchewan. And they have a great PhD program."

"Are you making that shit up?"

"No, really. I googled it."

He sits up a bit. "And there's nowhere more anonymous than the student housing ghettos."

"Yes, my man. That's what I'm talking about."

"We could do it."

I stand up and it feels like triumph already. "Yes, we could."

"All right," says JC, scootching over from the window seat to stand up beside me in the aisle. "What are we waiting for?"

"Nothing," I say, striding down the aisle toward the front. "Let's get out there and start our new lives." I step down onto the pavement and JC steps down beside me. We take a moment to look around the Sudbury Greyhound Station where even the blinking fluorescent

lights and the vomit stains on the sidewalk seem tinged
with hopefulness. Then four police officers step out from
around the front of the other bus.

"Watson Sinclair and JC Dubois — you are under
arrest."

And, just like that, our flight from justice is over.

twenty-three

At last, I'm where I belong. All my pigeons have come home to roost. My bad deeds have caught up with me and here I am, rotting away in the slammer, hoosegow, big house or whatever. The Sudbury Police Station. JC and I were together in a holding cell with a guy called Mike who had gotten drunk and put his car in a ditch, which is against the law and also going to play havoc with his insurance rates. I told him it would be cheaper for him to just fix his own damage, never tell his insurance company about the accident and hope they don't pull a random spot check on his MVR. He nodded and then knelt down in the corner for another round of the dry heaves, which made me feel like retching, too.

JC just sat in the corner watching Mike convulsing and me pacing around inside the cell. He kept himself to himself for the most part. We each called our wives with our phone calls and then we waited around all night for something to happen. We had a toilet, a sink, two metal bunks and a bench along one wall. Our gray cement block and poured concrete floor was a classic institutional decor scheme. The smell was a mingling of gym locker room with undertones of ass. Mike must have flushed well, for there were no acidic vomit notes.

It was impossible to sleep, so we paced up and down, sat around, lay around and otherwise killed time with our ammunition of remorse. I was suffering from some kind of time-bending hysterical fatigue, where I was jittery and near comatose at the same time. I thought, was this what jail was always going to be like? Four walls and a mind pulsating with fear trapped inside an incarcerated body? Then I thought, serves my mind right for coming up with such a stupid, stupid plan.

Early this morning, Mike was taken out for an appearance before a judge, flashing me the thumbs-up on the way by. As the guard slammed the cell door shut behind him, I thought, that might have been the last insurance advice of my career.

It was a couple of hours later by the time they finally came to get us and I thought we would be going in to face the judge also, but we both got taken to separate little rooms. I'm hanging out by myself. Just me and my roosting pigeons, metaphorically speaking. I've been in here for about an hour now, which is fine with me, because at least I'm not looking at iron bars. The walls are bare and the only thing in the room is a table with four chairs around it. I'm sitting here wishing I had a deck of cards or something. There's no two-way mirror in the room, but there is a camera up in the top corner near the ceiling tiles. Maybe the architect of the Sudbury jail never watches *Law & Order*, because I'm pretty sure the cops love an audience when they sweat a perp.

Maybe this is their way of making me sweat, just sitting by myself, wondering what's going to happen. But I know what's going to happen. Court appearance, public defender, trial, Kingston Pen. There is no mystery and here is as good as any place to hang out for now. Although I guess I am wondering if there will be some kind of extradition hearing and a plan to take us back to New York for trial on kidnapping and extortion charges. Oh, the possibilities. Canadian court or American court? Black and white stripes or blue coveralls?

The initial terror and sick feeling during our arrest hardened into a crystalline mass in the pit of my stomach over several hours and the ensuing dread and fearful anticipation cooled over time also. All I'm left with is mild depression and a sense of resignation to my fate. I lost it all the moment we put Ray in the back seat of my Honda, so it's been gone for a long time now. I notice that my teeth feel like they're wearing little sweaters because I haven't brushed them in something like twenty-four hours or so. At least I still have my sense of humor, which is always a valuable thing for someone whose life sucks as much as mine.

Speaking of sucking, the door opens and I hear the footsteps of the next chapter of my fate coming through the doorway and I'm almost too tired to care. I look up to see whether it is a cop or my lawyer, but of all the people I didn't expect to see, looking so beautiful and teary-eyed that it breaks my heart in a single second and makes me choke down a sob as I jump up to hug her, my Jessica was the biggest and best surprise I could have ever had.

"Honey," I say. Then I have to swallow again as I about bust out into sobs. I hug her and don't know what to say anyway, so I just hold her like that. I can't even look in her eyes, I feel so guilty. She is hugging me pretty tightly, so maybe forgiveness is an option. Maybe if I just keep on holding her, the hard feeling in my stomach will subside.

"Oh, sweetie," she says, finally, pulling away and holding my hand. "What an ordeal you've been through." Talking in this weird voice and looking meaningfully into my eyes as if I should get it. She leads me over and we sit down on opposite sides of the table, still holding hands and looking at each other and I have no idea what she's talking about. She looks up at the camera in the corner and then back at me and waits.

"Yes," I say. "It was… an ordeal." I raise my eyebrows, not knowing where to go from there. She takes the lead, which feels very normal.

"Ray explained everything to the FBI and the police."

Yes. And that is bad, right?

"He explained," she says with more emphasis. "How he was under a lot of deadline pressure and his doctor had told him he needed to take some time off. So he planned to keep a low profile by pretending to be sick and coming to visit you guys so you could help him work on the launch."

I nod thoughtfully. This sounds pretty good so far. Keep going.

She smiles at me and continues. "Because of the friendship you guys developed while you were corresponding about the comic strip over those many months. You agreed to help with the launch so he could take some time away from the office, which was driving him crazy."

Please God can this be true?

"So Gerald Spooner figured out that Ray wasn't at home, but he jumped to the wrong conclusion. Can you believe he actually thought you guys had kidnapped Ray?"

I realize I have been holding my breath and I let it out in one long flow and turn it into a whistle at the end. "Whew! That is crazy."

"You're telling me. The police even wanted to get a search warrant to check your parents' basement for

225

evidence," she says, giving me another meaningful look, which is starting to turn me on a little. "But after Ray explained everything, the judge was satisfied and he wouldn't authorize it."

Oh, I love this woman so much it hurts. I squeeze her hand and can't stop smiling, but I don't know where to go from here, so I keep quiet.

"We were all so worried about you when you guys took off that way, but Ray mentioned that you thought the police might want to charge you with fraud for pretending to be him while he was recuperating and that the whole launch would fall apart." She pauses and waits for me to catch up.

"Yes," I say. "Fraud. We were very worried about fraud... charges. Do you know that if I am convicted of a crime, I lose my RIBO license and I would never be able to act as an insurance broker again? It was tearing me apart. And JC was so scared of going to jail. We just got out of there. So, I guess they found my car in Woodstock?"

She smiles at that one. "Yes, and they had you on camera buying your tickets at the Greyhound station in Toronto."

"Hee-hee. No wonder they were waiting for us. Is Sylvie here, too?"

"Yes, she and I came up together. We drove all night. She's probably in talking to JC right now."

"Great. He'll be happy. So, are they going to press charges? On the fraud thing?"

"It looks like Ray has worked things out with Gerald Spooner and apologized for the subterfuge. He is taking responsibility for the deception, so we're just waiting for the police to finish the paperwork and we can go home."

"Oh, thank God!" I say. "I can't believe it's all over. I'm so sorry to have worried you. About everything." I give her a meaningful look, raising my eyebrows and offering a guilty half smile.

"We can talk about that later. Something else, though. You didn't make a statement to the police, did you?" She waits for my answer through clenched teeth.

"Are you kidding me? With all the TV and movies I've watched? I didn't even say hello."

She laughs at that and I have to get up and move around to her side of the table to kiss her, even if she's still mad at me. I just love her laugh. Surprisingly, she kisses me back.

"I have to apologize, too," she says after we unlock lips. "I wasn't very understanding about your crazy schedule the last couple of weeks. But I have some news about that. You might have noticed that I was a little bit… moody, at times? There is a reason for that. Are you sitting down?"

She can see I'm sitting down, so what the fuck?

"We're going to have a baby," she says. And she smiles wider than ever and squeezes my hand.

Pregnancy hormones! Fuck me, of course. "Oh, my God, Jess. A baby! That is such fantastic news." No wonder she was such a… that living with her was so… challenging. I hug her tightly, but at the same time, my brain is already working.

"I know," she says. "It all feels so weird. I was supposed to get my period the weekend you guys were in New York and I just thought I was late, but then this past weekend rolled around and still nothing. So I took a pregnancy test from the drugstore yesterday morning just before the police knocked on the door and I saw two lines.

I haven't been to the doctor, yet, because all this stuff has been happening."

"I can't believe I'm going to be a daddy."

"And I'm going to be a mommy, can you believe that?" She rests her head on my shoulder.

This is pure gold. Baby comics are always funny. *Family Circus, For Better or For Worse, Baby Blues…* we're going to be the next *Baby Blues*! This is awesome. If I start churning out the scripts about pregnancy issues and write a bunch about being a new dad, new baby stuff—I wonder how quickly JC can get to work and start hammering out some drawings?

"Watson? You're very quiet. What are you thinking?"

I pull back from our hug. "I was just thinking about this miracle of life that's growing inside you. Our baby. A little piece of you and me. A bit of our love coming into the world for us to treasure."

"Oh, my God. That's beautiful. I love you so much, honey."

"I love you." How quickly could we get this stuff off to the syndicates? I know Ray Bennett, now. Maybe he'd want to have first look at it. He knows the way we roll. The kind of determination we bring to a project.

"Maybe this will be a good thing for you," she says. "Nothing happens to us in this life that we don't learn from. This might allow you to let go of the dream of making it in comics — which, let's face it, was always a long shot — and let you settle down and focus on your job and on being a good daddy."

"I feel like I will be a good daddy." My brain is too stunned and fizzy inside to really take this in. I get the idea that a baby will come along and be in our lives, but it all just seems quaint. I'm picturing scenes of familial bliss in our house like glossies in a magazine. I'm sure the panic and insecurity will come later.

The door opens and one of the cops from before comes in. He gives me a kind of dirty look as if to qualify what he's about to say. "All right, Mr. and Mrs. Sinclair. Everything is in order. You're free to go now. You can collect your personal effects at the window on your right at the end of the corridor."

Jess stands up. "Thank-you, Officer King. And thanks for all your help."

"You're welcome." He steps aside to let us by, holding the door for us and everything.

"Thanks," I say. I grab my wife by the hand. "Honey, let's go home." We walk out of there together into the hallway and already I feel like a free man. This is it. This will be the best comic strip about baby stuff ever. And our muthafuckin' launch is gonna *blow up*. I can see it now. Get ready, world, because here we come. See you in the funny pages.

About the Author

Happily married since 1992 and a father since 2003, Mark has been a writer for as long as he can remember. He was born in Toronto and grew up in London, Ontario. He was the first winner of the *Lillian Kroll Prize for Creative Writing* at Western University, where he also completed a degree in English Literature. Mark has published novels, poetry, short fiction, feature articles, comic strips and book reviews in various media.

He lives in London with his wife and daughter, those to whom all his work and play is dedicated.

Connect with Mark at his website -
http://markvictoryoung.com/

For more comics by Levins & Young -
http://levinsandyoung.com/

Also from *Hanton House* by Mark Victor Young
Risk - a Novel

They're the most unlikely detectives.

Martin is a 38-year-old virgin marked for greatness by the insurance gods. In his professional life, he is paid to assess risk, but in his personal life he plays it safe. Experience has shown him that lonely is better than broken-hearted.

George is a wannabe architect with white man's dreadlocks. He risks his neck on the streets of Toronto every day as a bike courier, but his job is unchallenging and he chooses apathy over the risk of failure at what he really wants to do.

When George tags along with Martin to investigate the scene of his latest claim, they stumble upon a burglary in process. Now they are being hunted by an unknown adversary who will stop at nothing to get what he's after, forcing Martin and George into a dangerous game of cat and mouse in which they must risk everything.

Sample First Chapter

Martin Porchnik could see Jason from Claims approaching the Underwriting area with a yellow file in his hand and a big smirk on his face. A chill went through Martin, as it always did. A yellow file meant a property claim to be paid, and although he would ask not for whom the bell tolled, he still prayed it didn't toll for he.

"Good afternoon, 'Underwear' department. Whose day can I ruin today?" said Jason. "Anybody have a file for Ultimate Diecasting?"

Martin grimaced. He knew that name. Of all the shit files that landed in his lap, that one stuck out in his memory as one of the shittiest.

"Heads are going to roll over this one," said Jason, looking around with an evil grin.

"Not one of mine," said Darlene.

"It's not me," called Dave from his cubicle at the back.

"It's me," said Martin. Everybody looked at him and he shrugged his shoulders. What're ya gonna do?

"Is this the kind of crap you're writing down here?" Jason parked his bulk next to Martin's desk, leaning his elbow on the upper shelf. "No wonder I'm so busy paying out the big bucks. I need a dec page, underwriter boy."

He was what might be called a *big galoot*. Tallish and stocky going on fat with dark curly hair and thick eyebrows that looked angry or at least sarcastic all the time and a kind of goatee that made him look devilish.

"I haven't even issued the policy, yet," Martin said, looking away from Jason's dark eyes and back down at the yellow file that spelled possible doom. Did he have to enjoy it so much?

"Well, what's the hold up? Let's get it in gear. Do I have to come down here and crack the whip on you people?"

"It just came in last week." He dug through his pile of bound submissions waiting to be entered into the computer.

"Well, that didn't take long. What have you got for me, so I know how much I have to pay out here? Or did you want me to just give them a blank check?"

"We have a copy of their last year's dec page from the prior carrier. We bound coverage on the same basis." Well, he hadn't, but his boss had. The decs, or policy declarations, which were a listing of the coverages and wordings included, had just landed in his lap, in fact. And right away he had to hand them over to Jason so he could pay the first claim. Delightful.

"Gee, thanks. I guess it's something to go by. I'll make a copy, then."

"Can you leave me the claim file?"

"Sure. Read it and weep." Jason passed him the file and then walked away to the mail room to make his photocopy.

"Believe me, there will be tears," said Martin. He opened the file with a small feeling of self-satisfaction that he hoped wouldn't show on his face. He wasn't the one who had put them on the risk, so the blame wouldn't fully fall to him, come to that. It gave him a little get-out-of-jail-free card, but it was something he had to pretend he didn't think.

Underwriters spend most of every day considering risk. They read submissions of potential "risks," which in his department were businesses they were asked to insure. They had to assess the likelihood of having to pay out money because of some misadventure that might befall each. This would be some kind of lawsuit or a fire or a flood, etc. If you included famine, you would have almost all four horsemen of the Apocalypse. War is excluded. Underwriters choose which businesses to insure and how much money to charge so that, on average, a certain class of business would make money for the company.

The general principle of insurance is that the premiums of the many pay for the losses of the few. So they wrote up business for a whole lot of machine shops across Canada and only a few, like Ultimate Diecasting, would have a claim, and it should all even out and whatever was left over minus expenses was profit. If Martin did his job right.

So that is most of what underwriters do: consider which risks to get and which ones to keep by renewing. The rest of what they do all day is worry that the risks they have selected will have a big claim and they will be hauled onto the mat to answer for it. Consider risk and worry for a living. Nice work if you can get it. Martin shook his head and tried to concentrate on the claim report.

The date of loss was Sunday, so it had been the previous night. It was a professional hit. The line to the alarm monitoring station had been cut and the bars had been taken out along with the window, which was removed in one piece from the frame. The place was a mess and the only things missing were plans and blueprints from a current job. There would be a payout under "Valuable Papers" and a Business Interruption loss while the plans were reassembled. They would have to pay to have the line repaired and the window replaced.

Nothing else stolen or destroyed. That didn't sound right.

This one had disaster written all over it from the start. He remembered when the phone call had come in from the broker, only a week ago, and it hadn't passed the sniff test from the start.

"Hi, Martin. Listen, I've got a piece of new business for you. It's a machine shop. Do you think you could do it for four thousand bucks?"

"Let me take a look at it. Put some details on paper and fax it over."

"Can't you just quote me over the phone?"

"Well, what do they make?"

"Just various metal products."

"It makes a difference to what we would charge. And I'll also need construction and protection details on the building to determine the property rate."

"It's HCB, steel deck roof, of course. What else? I'm a busy man, Martin. I don't have time to get into all this detail."

"I can't quote over the phone. I'll need something in writing. Including receipts. Do they sell to the U.S.?"

"What do you think? Everybody sells to the U.S. This is just a little risk, I don't see the big deal."

"Sales to the U.S. increases our exposure. You'd better send something over."

"I'll get back to you."

Unbelievable, was his first thought when he had hung up the phone. What do we even need underwriters for if that's the way we're going to deal in insurance? It's not about the size of the building they occupy, or the number of people they have working for them, their level of training and qualification, or who they sell their products to, or how much they sell, or how much equipment they have and what it costs to replace it, would a key piece of equipment shut down the whole shop while it was being repaired, or whether they deal in cash or credit, or how long a fire would put them out of business, or ten or fifty other things that Jed Johansen wouldn't think to ask... it's about a few thousand bucks and a quick sale. Granted, 99% of brokers were diligent and professional and trustworthy, but it was the ones like Jed Johansen that you had to watch or else you ended up in situations like the one he was currently facing.

Jed never did send in a full quote submission, he just went over Martin's head and spoke to Gerry. "Gerry" was short for Geraldine, his supervisor. She preferred the diminutive, as she didn't live in the Victorian age. She was tall and confident and blond, and Martin found her easier to deal with than his previous boss. She had an intelligent face and sharp eyes. She was impatient all the time, but kind. From looking at the pictures on the desk of her husband and kids, he imagined she was one of those busy moms who were great with their kids, efficient at work and able to keep the whole world spinning on the end of a stick.

"I just got off the phone with one of the Johansen brothers, I forget which," Gerry had said when she dropped by his desk not twenty minutes after the first phone call came through. "I bound that risk, the machine shop, for $5000. He's faxing over last year's dec page."

"Oh," he had said hesitantly. This was very bad form, indeed. Without a written submission, there were no declarations or representations from the broker upon which to rely, and as they say, a verbal contract isn't worth the paper it's printed on, ha-ha.

"I know," said Gerry. "You're not happy about it."

Martin shrugged but looked steadily at her. "Not really. I don't like him bypassing me to get to you. You can't be doing all the quotes in the department."

"I know. It was an accommodation. This is a growth year, and we have got to take it where we can get it. Besides, we can get it inspected and take care of any problems then."

"When it will be too late to get more premium if we need it."

"It'll be fine, Martin. Besides, we're $5K to the good, instead of nothing, and I want to switch the Johansens on so they'll start sending us more business."

"I understand."

Five thousand dollars? They knew nothing about security, products, contracts, warranties... it would have to be inspected, thought Martin, just as the fax had been dropped off in his IN box.

It was out in Scarberia, their nickname for Scarborough, the north east part of Toronto. It was in a moderately high crime area, big limits on tools and computers, which were the first to go. This was terrible. The Total Insured Value, or TIV, was over $4 million: the company's money on the line for who knows what. And now a claim, proving him right about his fears.

"Here's your so-called dec page back." Jason loomed by his desk again. "Can I have my file back, or were you going to take it home with you?"

"It's all yours. Why do you think thieves would break into a place like that and not steal any tools or computers? Things with a quick turn around. Those are usually the first to go, and yet these thieves ignored them."

"What do you think, oh brainy one?"

"I think they knew what they were looking for. All

they took was highly specialized diagrams, plans, and design specs. What petty thief takes that?"

"Okay, so what?"

"It sounds suspicious, that's all. I think you should be careful with this one. It's bothered me since we wrote it."

"Well, thanks for the advice. I'm glad you know so much about how to do my job, because you obviously didn't know how to do yours."

"Hey, it was just a suggestion."

"I'll take it under advisement," said Jason over his shoulder.

When the adjuster had left, Martin quickly composed a fax form and fired it off to the broker: *Urgent. Insist that the insured upgrades security system to provide ULC-approved Line Security Level III protection, to prevent a recurrence of this kind of loss. Please advise ASAP how the insured intends to proceed. Our file is in abeyance pending your reply.* Then he walked over and knocked on Gerry's door.

"I know what you're going to say. I heard about it."

"I'm not going to say anything. I'm just wondering about this loss. It sounds suspicious to me. No tools or computers stolen. I still don't think we've got the whole story here, and that could mean non-disclosure. In which case we could VOID the policy *ab initio*."

"Marty. Get a grip. Bad losses happen to good underwriters. It's not your fault, and I know that. Leave the investigation to the Claims Department."

"Okay. I faxed the broker to get the line security in there or else face the hammer."

"That's all we can do. Now blow it off. You've had bigger losses than this. Besides, it builds character."

"It builds my stress level is what it does."

Leaving Gerry to her managing, he returned to his cube feeling dissatisfied. It was a mystery, that was for sure. But if he were reading this mystery in one of his detective novels, he would've put it down by now. Too boring. Something about this was not right, but it wasn't really his place to intrude. Let the Claims Department do their work. They were thorough, Jason's bluster notwithstanding. If there was something to find, they'd find it. Time to shake this off with a little caloric input.

He sat in the lunchroom quietly munching his sandwich. People came and went, mostly going back to eat at their desks, or going out for lunch. Martin was a fixture in the lunchroom: same time, same lunch, everyday. Lunch was about giving his mind a break. No magazines or TV, no conversation, no stimuli. It wasn't a Zen thing: be the sandwich, one hand clapping, or whatever. It just felt good to decompress and not think about anything, if he could manage it. Concentrate on the flavor of the sandwich and the chocolate bar.

It was the chocolate bars that gave him the spare tire, he felt, but he couldn't stop. They were an addiction. He was about 5'10", pudgy, especially around the gut. The old hairline was slowly retreating on him. At 38 years old, this was right on schedule, par for the genetic course. Thanks, Grandpa. But it didn't help that the media was always bombarding women with images of the ideal male, an ideal he couldn't live up to. Calvin Klein underwear ads had set his self-esteem back a pace, he could admit it now.

He poured another cup of coffee and went back to the cube. He tried to get back into the flow of things, but the stupid loss kept bugging him and he ended up just staring off into space for long periods of time, just trying to crack the code of this puzzle. That was how George, the bicycle courier who did their head office mail run every day found him, lost in thought at his desk.

"Hey, buddy," he said, picking up the name plate on his desk and flipping it over in his hand, tapping it on the desk. "Where's my envelope?"

"Hey, go easy on the name plate."

"Sorry about that. I don't want to break the last link to your sense of identity."

"Don't worry, my name's sewn into the backs of all my shirts."

"There you go. You'll be fine."

"All right, just let me collect it up." Martin got up out of his chair, glad for something else to think about and a chance to shoot the breeze with George. He had been doing the pick-ups at their office for a few years now and he and Martin had been out for drinks a couple of times after work. He was a good guy, despite his scary appearance. Tall, sunglasses, white man's dreadlocks, tattoos, pierced this and that... he wasn't like Martin's insurance friends, but that's what he liked about him. He was different.

"No rush. I'm ahead of schedule today," said George.

George came with him into the mail room, and talked to him as he gathered up all the envelopes, memos, and various other correspondence, packaged and weighed it all, and wrote out the receiving slip.

"So, rough day, or just hungry?" said George.

"It's been one of those days. Started out okay, but it all went quickly downhill this afternoon."

"Sounds like a pretty normal Monday."

"Yeah, I guess. Well, here it is. Signed, sealed, and

now just to be delivered."

"Thanks. We going for drinks tonight, Marty?"

"Not tonight, but maybe some night this week."

"Just say the word." George put on his sunglasses as Martin walked him out through the office and over to the main door.

"Bye, George," called Janice.

"Bye." The door closed behind him.

"Whew, he's cute," said Janice. "Do you know if he's single?"

"Um, yes. I mean, yes, I do know he lives with his girlfriend."

"Too bad. Such a hottie! He can deliver my package anytime."

Janice was a bit of a hottie herself, in that secretary way. Single secretaries exude this air of availability and eagerness, like bridesmaids. She was no supermodel, which Martin didn't mind. That type of woman intimidated Martin, anyway. They always looked so severe, so hard, with angry-looking cheek bones. He always imagined them as martial arts experts, capable of knocking his block off if he so much as looked at them.

No, she was solidly built, pretty, and seemed fun to be around. Shoulder length blond hair-product hair, small features, fair-sized bust and hips. Looking very fertile. In her early 30's, he guessed. But she would probably say no. Look at him. Why would she go out with him? He wasn't much to look at. And even if they did go out once or twice, something would happen and the whole thing would go to hell and it would hurt like the last time he got involved with someone. Then he wouldn't be able to look her in the eye at work the next morning. Always have to pretend to check out the paint job on the walls as he walked by her desk. And face the shame of a failed office romance. It wasn't worth it.

Quietly back across the office, shy glance around, wishing he could turn himself invisible, wanting to escape people's notice and make it back to the safety of his little cube without anyone confronting him. Feeling strangely persecuted, as if everyone were against him. Couldn't seem to face anything or anyone right now.

--

For further details or to purchase a copy of *Risk,* please visit http://markvictoryoung.com/risk/.

Also from *Hanton House* by Mark Victor Young
***Once Were Friends* - a Novel**

If you think it's hard to win back the one that got away, try doing it while you're taking over her family's company.

To save the firm his father built, ambitious CEO **Hal Mercer** has to initiate a hostile takeover of industry giant D'Arville Industries.

Owned by the family of the only woman he's ever loved, **Kate D'Arville** certainly isn't going to stand by and let him destroy her family's empire. If only she'd have dinner with him, he could make her understand his intentions. If Hal fails, it's his family's company that's doomed, his employees who'll lose their jobs. He can't let that happen, but Hal isn't used to having everyone counting on him like this.

Problem is, it's becoming less clear which is more important to him—winning the corporate battle of his life or the heart of the woman he loves.

Sample First Chapter

They were pinned down under heavy fire in the empty shell of what had looked like a partially burned-out general store. Hal Mercer crouched below a windowless frame on the second floor, listening for footsteps on the stairs. *Damn! Now his mask was fogging up.* He tried to wipe it with one finger, hearing shouts in the smoky air as the enemy crawled up their unprotected flank, the heavy *Phut! Phut! Phut!* of sniper fire covering their approach. Where the hell did he go from here?

Hal glanced out the window. Abandoned car wrecks covered with spray paint lined the street in front of the building, stacks of tires lay toppled at the curb, obscure suggestions of movement over there told him that enemy positions were advancing along the tree line to his right, and then the sound of two slugs slamming into the window frame next to his ear made him duck back under the ledge. Raising his gun over the ledge for a moment, he squeezed off a round in the general direction of the trees.

"Archie?" he shouted off into the darkness to his left.

"Yes, *mon capitaine?*"

"You see those guys coming up by the trees?"

A pause. "Yes, sir."

"Can you create a diversion on your side to draw their fire?"

"I'm on the case, sir."

Archie was playing some kind of game, obviously. He wasn't this good at taking orders and he also hated Hal intensely. He would be more likely to stab Hal in the back

246

than cover it for him.

"Go ahead, then," Hal yelled.

Then a shuffling noise from the next room and several shots followed by a wet *SLAP*, and Archie Bishop's voice shouting, "I'm hit, I'm hit! They got me, captain!"

Hal's heart was pounding in his chest as he reviewed his options. With Archie out, he was likely all alone here on the second floor, with who knew how many of his division gone. Going outside would be suicide, as he could see from the figures advancing on all sides, but staying here only delayed the inevitable.

Then there was a squeak from behind him, and the sound of a careful footstep on the stairs, and Hal, keeping low under the window, crawled to the darkened corner at the far end of the room, his weapon pointed at the top of the stairs. The dark shape of a head bobbed into view, eyes trained along the barrel of a gun that scanned left and right like a periscope on an emerging submarine. Then more of the body came into view: an absurdly tall, hunched-over figure with sticking-out ears and ridiculous fatigues—it was Johnson from Accounting.

"Die, pencil-pusher," said Hal as he squeezed the trigger, firing a single round into Johnson's midsection.

"Ow!" said Johnson. "I'm hit."

The adrenaline rush was amazing! Oh, well. Nothing left to lose. Hal scurried to the window and started firing at anything and everything that moved. "Banzai! This one's for Archie." He caught someone hurrying across the street in front of him and quickly fired a couple of rounds in that direction. A woman's voice called out, "I'm hit," just as he caught sight of the tiny yellow orb coming at him, seemingly growing larger as it descended along its shallow arc, and exploding on contact with his visor. Shaking his head from the surprising force of the impact, he couldn't quite shake off the darkness of the thick paint obscuring his view.

Hal shouted, "I'm hit," and sank back blindly onto the floor to wait for the whistle. He had been killed yet again, but he couldn't help smiling. Who knows what it was doing for morale, but he was having the most fun he'd had in ages. Why had it taken him so long to discover the joy of paint ball? He felt good about the way the Senior Management team rallied around him, even if they had lost two of their three engagements. What the heck, at worst it was something different for everyone to do on a weekend that was on the company tab.

Okay, sure, he wasn't that "easy come, easy go" about it. He had spent weeks planning this event and was desperately hoping everyone was having fun. And morale simply had to improve; it couldn't get much worse. It was a tough time for the company now and if he was going to achieve what he wanted—no, scratch that—what he had to achieve, then he had to make some changes for the better.

Was he the only one who worried about this stuff?

Right. Sniff, sniff. It's lonely at the top.

* * *

"Okay, troops. Let's bring it in," said Bill Fluellen, the section manager, as they were milling around in the lobby. Pete Malden rolled his eyes. Another management speech. Didn't he get enough of this during the work week? He looked over at Fluellen. His boss was an imposing figure even when he wasn't dressed in military fatigues. His thick red hair and salt and paprika goatee was flecked with sweat and sawdust.

"We did great out there," he was saying. "We worked together and really stuck it to those wallies from the IT crew. Malden and Bardolph, way to cover each other. Where's Bardolph?"

"Right here, sir. Ten-hut!" Randy Bardolph snapped to attention behind his boss in a mock salute.

"At ease. You were quite the drama queen with your little 'death scene' out there."

"Sorry, sir. Next time I give up my life for you in battle, I'll try to go with more dignity."

"Excellent. Bottom line, we came together as a team and defended our position despite overwhelming odds. As your commanding officer, I was damn proud to lead you onto the field. That's the last exercise of the day, so I'll just say enjoy the rest of your weekend, and I'll see you back at the office Monday morning."

Pete sat on a low bench against the wall and covered his nose with his sleeve as the pervasive combined aroma of stale sweat, cigar smoke and something moldy mingled with the fresh body odors filling the room. Randy, Amy, and Arthur sat or stood next to him.

"Pete, I love the blue hair," said Amy, smoothing her own hair behind both ears with her fingertips. "You should really keep it like that." Her dark hair was in a short bob kept away from her face. She had a mostly slim and petite frame, so her navy sweatshirt with the George Brown College logo hung a bit too loosely from her shoulders, but her curvy hips filled out her dark olive army pants so she didn't just look skinny.

He liked being able to see this casual side of her.

Even on dress down day she wasn't like this, preferring business casual to jeans and a T-shirt. Those army pants were driving him wild. He wondered if they could somehow make paint ball a weekly thing.

Pete caught her eye and then ran his fingers through the blue patch of hair and looked away. "Yeah, thanks. My version of a battle scar. 'It's a far better thing I do than I have ever done', one life to give for the department and all that."

"So what are we supposed to feel now? A stronger sense of team cohesion?" said Randy. "Or do you find yourself with even more questions about the people you work with?"

"Yeah," said Arthur. "Like what was with those IT geeks who had their own guns?"

"Scary," said Pete. "And some were like automatics or something."

"I have a picture in my mind," said Randy, applying two fingers to his right temple and closing his eyes, his mouth pursed in a little smirk. He was what you might call portly, but with a dignified air and busy hands with long fingers that were animated when he talked and drumming or tapping when he was listening. He cleared his throat. "They are here every weekend, keeping track of their 'kill-shots,' have a full set of military fatigues—no offence, Amy—have no girlfriends, live in their parents' basements which smell exactly like this place, and they're each composing the ultimate online game to ensure their places in history."

Amy put a hand on her hip. "The only reason I have these army pants is because they were in fashion for about 10 minutes when I was in grade 12, and this is the only place I've had a chance to wear them since then, and when's the last time you had a girlfriend, Randy?"

"Touché," said Randy.

"I think you make a cute military chick," said Pete.

"Thank-you, Peter." She smiled at him.

"Yeah, I was going to say that, too, Amy," said Arthur. "I noticed the same thing."

Pete looked at his rival. Shit, that's all he needed. Not that Arthur was much competition. He was tall and thin with a generally hunched posture that looked a bit like he was trying to brace himself for impact. Inexplicably, he was wearing a blue oxford cloth button down and beige cotton chinos, as if he were off to a college mixer of yesteryear, albeit they were now tie-dyed with paint splotches. Did they have college mixers in the Summer of Love?

Amy gave Arthur a suspicious look. "There's no way I'm doing your reconciliation for you next week so you can forget it."

"No, I wouldn't, I just…" said Arthur.

Randy patted Arthur on the shoulder. "Of course you wouldn't, Arthur. Did anybody catch sight of our fearless leader? He was supposed to be here today."

"Hal? No, but I would love to know who shot him," said Pete.

"We'll hear about it Monday, I'm sure," said Amy.

"I'm surprised we didn't get a speech from the little general," said Randy.

"Which unit just squared off with the S&M team?" asked Arthur, using their secret code for the Senior Management group.

"I think it was Marketing, and you know they'd lie down and play dead rather than smoke the big bosses," said Pete, leaning back against the wall and folding his arms across his chest. "They know which side their bread is buttered." He had a slim build and wore black jeans and a long sleeve red t-shirt with a Spider-Man symbol surrounded by webs on the front. His blue eyes and long lashes were the occasional envy of the women in his life, but his normally dark and not blue hair was short and messy-on-purpose.

"They're smart. You've got to learn to play politics with the management types if you ever want to become one." Amy made a nose plugging gesture and craned her neck to see over the crowd. "Geez, it smells. Is that line getting any shorter? I'd really like to get out of here."

"I know," said Pete. "I feel like the smell is in my mouth now. I might just need a cold beer to counteract it."

* * *

"So whose idea was it to do this whole team-building paint ball thing, anyway?" said Arthur as they sat around a table at *The Fletcher's Quiver* Pub. They had a booth to the right of the bar, slightly toward the back. Pete surveyed the room and the various Robin Hood artifacts above their heads.

"Well, what else can you think of that's new around the office?" said Randy.

"Yeah, I know Hal is the new CEO, but do you really think it was his idea?"

"Of course it is. When you're the new guy, you have to come in and piss on the bushes, mark your territory," said Randy. "This is just one of many new things still to come, and not all of them will be good, just wait."

"But it was his father's company," said Arthur. "Why would he want to change things so much? I mean, doesn't that reflect poorly on his dad?"

"More likely he wants it to reflect well on him," said Pete.

"Yes, our boy does have a reputation to live down," said Randy. "He was the biggest shit disturber of all of us when he worked the floor with Pete and me."

"Wow," said Arthur.

Randy and Pete exchanged an uncomfortable glance, remembering somebody was missing. A year earlier, they would have been here with Hal, talking about the very people he was probably out for drinks with right now.

Thursday nights after work were what Hal had dubbed "group therapy" sessions at the local watering hole. There were always five to ten of them from the office, a revolving door of old pros, new hires who looked promising and the core group of Hal, Pete and Randy. Hal would get Randy going about something and then he would hold court while Hal bought a round of *B-52s* or *Sexes on the Beach* or something and hit on the waitresses. Pete would draw pictures of the senior managers or supervisors and they would end up eating chicken wings for their dinner around 10 o'clock and then close out the bar. Pete and Randy would stumble onto the subway and Hal would grab a taxi going the other way, often with female companionship in tow.

For about the last six months it had been just Pete and Randy. After Arthur had joined their section, he had come out once in a while, but their get-togethers had become less frequent since Hal had ascended the top of the org chart. The dynamic was somewhat flat without him.

"Yeah," said Pete. "And before he surprised everyone and came to work with us, he did the whole life of leisure, rich kid, country club. We heard all the stories, believe me."

Randy nodded agreement while he finished a sip of his martini. "My uncle golfed at his club and knew him well. Hal would spend all day on the golf course. An excellent golfer, I'm told."

"I'll bet he was a hit with the ladies," said Amy. "With that rock star hair and those dark eyes... mmm, yummy."

"You have a woody for our CEO?" said Pete. "Ewww. Now I know how you plan to get to the top."

"He can heighten my, um, future prospects any time." Amy smiled at all of them.

"Quite," said Randy. "But you notice the rock star hair was gone before the board meeting when they voted on his coronation? And he actually went out and bought his first suit. Our boy Hal has really grown up."

"I'm sure he had his suit and haircut before the funeral," said Pete. The others all nodded and found it was a good time to have a sip of their drinks and inspect their surroundings. Pete looked down at the Robin Hood caricature he'd been doodling on a spare bar mat, picked it up and shook it to dry the ink. "But I'll give you this: he was the laziest one of any of us on the fifteenth floor."

"Hear, hear," said Randy. He looked at his watch. "Well, I think it's time I moved on. Do you still need a ride?" He touched Arthur's arm.

"Yeah," said Arthur, sucking back the last of his beer.

Randy indicated the half full glasses in front of them. "Are you guys staying on?"

"I'm just going to finish this beer," said Pete.

"Me, too," said Amy.

"Right. See you Monday." Randy waved and walked to the front door and out, followed closely by Arthur.

Pete smiled and had a casual sip of his drink. "Sorry, I didn't mean to break up the party."

"You didn't," said Amy. "It was just one of those pauses in the conversation. And I think Randy was realizing he sounded a little full of himself."

"Doesn't he always?"

"Let's see how you're coming along with Robin Hood. Hey, pretty good likeness of Hal, there. Is he an anti-Robin? The rich stealing from the poor?"

"Isn't that what the rich always do? No, I just felt like putting his head on a Robin Hood body. Inspired by my surroundings."

Amy nodded. "It's really good."

"Thanks. So what did you think of today, really?"

"I liked it. As corny as it sounds, it does build team spirit. It lets us have a little fun and see a different side of the people we work with, and I would never have tried it otherwise."

"Yeah, I guess so. But requiring us to give up most of our Saturday for a work function kinda bugs me."

"I work plenty of Saturdays as it is."

"Yeah, but that's different. It's voluntary. I don't know, it just rubs me the wrong way. Do I really want to socialize with the people I work with? Don't I see them enough with, what, 45% of my waking hours spent at work already?"

"Should I be offended?"

"I didn't mean you, and you know it."

"Hey, you could've got a doctor's note."

"I know. Ignore me, I'm just lipping off. So what do you have planned for tonight? Any hot date on the horizon?"

"A hot date with my laundry is all."

"What, no boyfriend for the great Amy Quick, after giving Randy a hard time this afternoon over his lack of female companionship?"

"I don't think Randy craves female companionship. And no, neither of us has a boyfriend."

"Whaaat? You think Randy's gay? Just because he doesn't have a girlfriend? Does that make me gay, too?"

"No, with you I can't see it. But Randy has a quality, as they say." She paused and looked towards the door. "He never really talks about his social life, does he?"

"I, let me think… Who did he go on vacation with that time? Down south?"

"My point exactly. A friend is all he said."

"All right, maybe. I don't know. So what if he is?"

"I just like to ride him a little bit. See if I can shake his unflappable reserve."

"But you're not going to cause any embarrassing scenes? I prefer 'don't ask, don't tell,' if we could just keep it at that."

"Oh, I'm not going to out him, don't worry. Now what have you drawn there?"

"Oh, this." He shook the bar mat dry again and showed her the second figure.

She took it and peered at it while holding it to face the light. "What is that? Is that Randy as a cat?"

"That's Randy as a player in Cats."

"Oh, I get it. A Broadway musical." She smiled and put it back down on the table.

"Yes, I guess you've poisoned my mind now, and I will never be able to think of him without thinking that."

"You know what they say about homophobes…"

"No, I don't. And I don't want to know. Not that I think that way. I'm fine with it."

Amy nodded and sipped her drink down to the ice cubes.

"So what happened with, I think his name was Joey, or Joe?"

"What?"

"The old boyfriend? Now no longer."

"Oh, yeah. Well, I guess we were both so busy with work, we were just seeing each other less and less. I'm still doing the night school classes, so it was hard to even get a free night that we could get together. So I said let's quit it and save ourselves a painful break-up."

"Right. That's grounds for a painful break-up right there."

"He was okay. Relieved, almost. We both realized it wasn't going anywhere, I think."

"You think."

"You don't know Joe. He works longer hours than I do."

"Mmm."

"Well, it's getting to be that time." She looked around for a clock. "My dirty clothes beckon."

"Yeah, I guess I'll get going, too. Where are you parked?" He shimmied down to the end of the bench and stood.

"Right out front," she said, standing. "Where are you?"

"Not far." They walked around the front of the bar and out the main door to the sidewalk. Pete pointed back down the road towards the *Paint War!* building. "Back the way we came. About a block back, there. The red one."

"Okay, well, see you Monday." She smiled and squinted into the light.

"See you Monday. Right." He did a sort of wave, and half turned towards his car.

Amy produced a key fob from her purse and aimed it at a car, pressing a button that made the car's lights flash. She walked around to the driver's side and opened the door. "Bye."

He nodded. "Bye."

Pete walked down the sidewalk towards his car, not looking back in case she was watching to see if he looked back. No more boyfriend. This was fantastic. He hadn't lied about her military outfit—he was hot for her in those clothes. He had, of course, always noticed her tight little body and always felt a bit of the tease in the way she looked at him and talked to him. Now that there was no boyfriend in the picture, it was all about strategy. Time to make his move. He would have to deal with Arthur, of course, but that would wait until Monday.

It was a cool fall day, slightly overcast. He drove home with the windows down and his music turned up, smiling at nothing. Home was a one-bedroom apartment in the Danforth, Toronto's Greektown area. It was sparsely furnished, had a cabinet full of movies, and everywhere boxes and boxes of comics. Various framed superhero posters by his favorite artists decorated the walls.

The kitchen table was also his drawing board for his own drawings, most of which were of the superhero or heroine variety. His Saturday night consisted of a heated can of ravioli eaten at the table while working on a large-scale Batman scene, with the original Batman movie, the one with Jack Nicholson as The Joker, playing in the background for atmosphere.

There used to be more furniture, and some throw pillows, and tasteful decorative prints on the walls, and no room for any of his things in the bathroom, but that stuff had been gone for some time now. Now there was more room for his comics, and he could leave the boxes all over the place and no one complained.

At the same time, he missed the other stuff.

--

For further details or to purchase a copy of *Once Were Friends*, please visit http://markvictoryoung.com/once-were-friends/